Search for the
Hidden Garden

A Discovery
with Saint Thérèse

By Sherry Weaver Smith

Pauline
BOOKS & MEDIA
Boston

Library of Congress Cataloging-in-Publication Data

Names: Smith, Sherry Weaver, 1969- author. | Thornburgh, Rebecca McKillip, illustrator.

Title: Search for the hidden garden : a discovery with Saint Thérèse / written by Sherry Weaver Smith ; illustrated by Rebecca Thornburgh.

Description: Boston, MA : Pauline Books & Media, [2016] | Summary: "A young girl is influenced by her friendship with St. Thérèse and her search for a hidden garden in the forest"—Provided by publisher.

Identifiers: LCCN 2015027480 (print) | LCCN 2015038584 (ebook) | ISBN 9780819890504 (pbk.) | ISBN 0819890502 (pbk.) | ISBN 9780819890511 (epub)

| ISBN 9780819890528 (mobi) | ISBN 9780819890535 (pdf)

Subjects: LCSH: Thérèse, de Lisieux, Saint, 1873–1897—Juvenile fiction. | CYAC: Thérèse, de Lisieux, Saint, 1873–1897—Fiction. | Gardens—Fiction. | Catholics—Fiction. | Christian life—Fiction. | Mystery and detective stories.

Classification: LCC PZ7.1.S656 Se 2016 (print) | LCC PZ7.1.S656 (ebook) | DDC [Fic]—dc23

LC record available at http://lccn.loc.gov/2015027480

This is a novelized story including Saint Thérèse of Lisieux. While Saint Thérèse is a real historical figure, elements of this story—including other characters, conversations, the plot, and events—are fictional products of the author's imagination.

Cover design by Putri Mamesah (novice, Daughters of St. Paul)

Illustrations by Rebecca Thornburgh

Published by Pauline Books & Media, 50 Saint Paul's Avenue, Boston, MA 02130–3491

Printed in the U.S.A.

SFHG SIPSKOGUNKYO3-21050 9050-2

www.pauline.org

Pauline Books & Media is the publishing house of the Daughters of St. Paul, an international congregation of women religious serving the Church with the communications media.

1 2 3 4 5 6 7 8 9   20 19 18 17 16

To my daughter, Laura Joan Smith,
and to my inspirations for this story:
my mother, Cheryl Lynn Weaver;
my late uncle, David George Davis;
and my sister, Kristin Weaver Samuelson

Contents

People and Places

Who you will meet in this story

Charlotte Masson (shar-LOT mah-SON)
> A ten-year-old girl who would like to go on an adventure

Anne
> Charlotte's best friend

Sister Saint Francis
> A teacher and nun at Charlotte's school

Louise Bouchard (boo-SHARD)
> A classmate of Charlotte and Anne

Thérèse Martin (teh-REHZ)
> A fifteen-year-old girl soon entering a monastery—a place for nuns to live, work, and pray

Madame Masson (ma-DAHM mah-SON)
> Charlotte's mother

Madame Bouchard (ma-DAHM boo-SHARD)
> Louise's mother

Monsieur Jean-Marc Dubois (miss-YEEUH ZHAHN-MARK doo-BWAH)
> The gardener for the Bouchard estate

Elena (EL-en-ah)

A maid for the Bouchard estate who also watches over Monsieur Dubois

Olivier Bernard (oh-LI-vee-ay bear-NARD)

Charlotte's ten-year-old friend who does not attend her school

Marc

Olivier's six-year-old younger brother

Vincent

Louise's older brother who is twelve-years old

Theo (TAY-oh)

Charlotte's six-year-old younger brother

Monsieur Bouchard (miss-YEEUH boo-SHARD)

Louise's father and a wealthy businessman

Inspector Dufour (an-spek-TOR due-FOOR)

A police detective

Monsieur Masson (miss-YEEUH mah-SON)

Charlotte's father

Where and when this story takes place

This story takes place in the town of Lisieux in northern France. The region around Lisieux is called Lower Normandy. The time is the spring of 1888.

What you will encounter in this story

Baguette (bag-ET)
> a long, thin, and crusty loaf of bread

Carmel (car-MEL), Carmelite (CAR-muh-lite)
> Carmelites can be men or women. Carmelite women, called sisters, serve God by living together in monasteries called Carmels. Inside the gardens and walls of the monastery, they help the world by praying and working. Carmelite sisters spend hours of each day praying alone as well as together.

Copybook
> a blank book for notes or homework, usually for writing examples over and over again. Students often used copybooks for handwriting and math.

Estate
> a mansion, which is a big house, surrounded by a large area of land.

Madame (mah-DAHM)
> the French word for Mrs.

Monastery
> a place where men or women live, work, and pray together to serve God.

Monsieur (miss-YEEUH)
> the French word for Mr.

A Treasure Map

~ 1 ~

"Disruptive," the teacher said as she wrote on the blackboard. "Write it in your copybook. It is your first spelling word."

All of the girls dipped their pens into the ink-wells on their desks. With one tap, they each shook off the extra ink and began to write—everyone but Charlotte Masson.

Charlotte wished that she could drift away like the white feather floating away from her desk. But she wasn't on an adventure, at least not yet. Instead, she was sitting in a classroom in a town in northern France.

She made one dot and stopped. Charlotte planned to start some "disruptive" trouble at any minute. Her mother wouldn't be happy if she misbehaved. But this time, it would be for a good reason. She just *had* to take a closer look at the map she'd seen in the library the day before. Charlotte's plan was to get in trouble so that she would have to clean the library as a punishment. It was the only way she could think of to see the map alone.

"Discovery. Think of finding something wonderful," the teacher said. "The next word is . . ." *Something wonderful*, Charlotte thought, *like the map in the library. It might even be a treasure map!*

Charlotte's teacher was a nun, or a religious sister. She wore a long black dress with a white triangle bib and a black veil on her head. Charlotte jumped in her seat when her teacher tapped a pointer stick on her desk. *She can't know that I'm up to something, can she?* thought Charlotte.

There was a rustling sound off in the corner where the students' satchel bags hung like soldiers at attention.

"Discover . . . ?" Sister Saint Francis repeated by mistake. Charlotte looked at the satchels out of the corner of her eye. All of the other girls turned their heads, all except Charlotte's best friend, Anne.

Anne looked right at Charlotte. In response Charlotte shrugged so hard her shoulders almost hit her ears. She didn't want Anne to get in trouble, too. The sounds stopped until . . .

A crash came from the frosted glass windows on the other side of the room. Something was scraping and trying to break in. Then, a fluffy, white shape fluttered up and down outside the window.

A squeak came from the corner. A number of chirps followed fast.

The white shape at the window clucked. Looking pale, Anne stood up. "I think that there might be a hen outside our window. But why it's knocking on the glass, I don't know . . ."

Suddenly, a ball of yellow burst out of Charlotte's satchel. A few feathers floated after it. A terrified chick skittered this way and that.

Charlotte reached down and scooped up the chick with her hands. But the bird knew how to break out of eggs and bags—and hands, too. It pecked so hard that Charlotte had to let go. The chick scrambled down to her desk and ran across her paper.

Flapping wings much smaller than its round body, the chick fluttered over to the desk of Louise Bouchard. The little bird's foot landed right in a blob of ink. Over and over, the chick stamped Louise's work—"disruptive, discovery"—with spiky prints.

Charlotte had not planned for this.

What would her teacher say?

〜 2 〜

"This, this *thing* is ruining my spelling!" Louise wailed. Sister Saint Francis tried to herd the chick with her long skirt.

"We must stay calm so we can catch the chick," Anne said. Dressed like a scary crow, the nun just made the little bird run faster.

"Stay calm!" girls shouted, in anything but a calm way. The hen flapped her wings and hovered outside.

Charlotte crept closer to the chick and opened her hands to form a bowl. "Come on," she whispered. "Thank you for creating a disruption. Now, let's get you out of here." With a stretched neck, the little bird stepped up into her hand.

Anne opened the door to the outside. Charlotte led the hen, stabbing at her heels, to the fence between the schoolyard and the next-door farm. She dropped the chick on the other side, and it fluttered down like a little falling patch of sunshine. The hen followed, flapping over the fence.

When Sister Saint Francis asked where the chick had come from, Louise said she had seen it come out of Charlotte's satchel. *Of course, Louise would tell on me*, thought Charlotte. *It's not like Louise is my friend.* But when the teacher said Charlotte was in trouble, she could hardly keep from smiling.

As Charlotte had hoped, her punishment was to clean the library. The chick had done her part. Charlotte even got some of the hen's feathers to add to a grand hat she planned to make.

As her classmates went to recess, Charlotte burst into the empty library. Even on a bright day, the library was a mysterious place. The top shelves were so high that it seemed like a forest of books. Charlotte could never read all their pages, just like she could never see the tops of all the trees in a forest.

Charlotte spotted a piece of paper on top of some books. There it was—the map—right next to the globe and near an open Bible. Alone in the library, she rushed over to look at the paper.

She had seen the map from far away when she'd visited with her whole class. Now she could look at it up close. Charlotte read the words aloud:

"Garden for Children.
Enter at the door near the flowers
that are the color of dawn.
To complete the mission,
find the four hidden fruit trees!
Follow four white stone paths,
one for each tree.
Careful! Ferns, leaves, and pine needles
might have covered up the paths.
On the stones, I've painted different kinds of fruit.
You must find four fruit trees:
apricot, clementine, red currant, and pear."

A mission! An adventure! Charlotte studied the map. It showed a stone wall that circled a large garden full of leafy trees and evergreens. There was only one door. *That must be the way in,* Charlotte thought. The mapmaker had added a small group of flowers there. *Are those the color of dawn?* Charlotte wondered. *What color could that be? Mysterious!*

Right after the door, the map showed a path of yellow flowers inside the garden. She read again, "Follow four white stone paths, one for each tree." The map didn't show the stone paths, only the flower path. And it didn't show the hidden fruit trees either. *Finding the paths and trees must be part of the mission,* she thought. *I'll have to find them myself.*

She wondered also about the painted fruits on the stones. *What were these different kinds of fruit? Also mysterious!*

In the center of the map, the word "treasure" was written inside a pear.

Charlotte almost cheered. But she couldn't. She was in the library. Right then and there, however, she decided that she would complete the mission by finding the four hidden fruit trees. Charlotte would become the most adventurous girl in the school— much more adventurous than Louise Bouchard!

Then Charlotte noticed something else. At the bottom of the map, the mapmaker had signed his name:

> Jean-Marc Dubois, Master Gardener,
> the Bouchard Estate.

"*Bouchard.*" Charlotte wrinkled her nose. The gardener worked for Louise's family. She didn't want Louise to know about the map, but she'd have to find a way to talk to the gardener.

For now, Charlotte would keep the whole thing quiet. She went to check the window. Across the abbey school's meadow, Charlotte didn't see anyone, only a grove of trees. She closed a large panel, like the cover of a book, over the glass, and left the darkened library.

$$\sim 3 \sim$$

When Charlotte was almost finished cleaning, her stomach began to hurt. She looked at a statue of Mary, the Mother of Jesus, on a shelf in the hallway. What would her own mother do when she found out about the chick? Her mother wanted her to be more like Thérèse Martin, who had been a top student at the school. Charlotte got a few wildflowers she had picked that morning. She dusted around the statue and put the flowers at the bottom.

She heard footsteps, but it wasn't Sister Saint Francis. It was someone coming from the chapel: Thérèse. The older girl had left the school a few years before, but everyone knew who she was. Thérèse sometimes visited the school chapel to pray. Everyone liked her because she was so kind. Thérèse, like Charlotte, had been a day student, who didn't live at the school.

"Good afternoon, Thérèse. I'm Charlotte."

Thérèse smiled. She was five years older than Charlotte, who was ten, and much taller. She seemed to walk everywhere with a purpose.

Charlotte said, "Is it true that you are going to Carmel to become a nun? Don't nuns pray all the time?" Everyone was talking about how Thérèse was going to enter the convent soon, even though she was only fifteen. Once inside, she would no longer be allowed to walk around the town. She would simply stay there and pray.

"Well, yes," said Thérèse warmly, "You see, Carmelite sisters pray and stay inside a monastery. Other types of sisters, like your teacher, Sister Saint Francis, pray but also work outside in schools or hospitals. I want to serve Jesus and pray as much as I can, so I am becoming a Carmelite."

"But I heard no one ever comes out of there! I could *never* do something like that. Praying is a good thing, but praying *that* much would be boring."

"Boring?" Thérèse asked, smiling.

As fast as a chick could disrupt a classroom, Charlotte knew she should have kept silent. Thérèse's family was probably proud of her. Not like Charlotte's mother. Charlotte felt her face redden.

"Did you get in trouble today, Charlotte?" Thérèse said. She must have noticed Charlotte's face.

"Yes, I did. I'm worried my mother will be upset. But it was for a good reason . . ."

"Everyone makes mistakes, Charlotte."

"It wasn't exactly a mistake. But I'm sure you don't make any."

"Of course I make mistakes. Once I asked my family's maid to get an inkstand down from a shelf on the fireplace. She was tall and I was too small to reach it. She said she wouldn't do it, so I dragged over a heavy chair. It scraped on the floor, and I stomped my feet. I even shouted at her that *she* was a brat. My older sister told me to say I was sorry. But I wasn't. Not at all."

Charlotte laughed. "How old were you?"

"Maybe eight? Jesus understands our mistakes. Just as the sun shines on every plant in the forest, his love reaches everyone. Just try to do as many small, good things as you can."

"But I'm in big trouble. It might take a lot of very big things to balance that out."

Thérèse pointed to the statue of Mary. "It looks like you put flowers there. Maybe you pray and do more good than you think. I'll ask Jesus to help you and your friends discover many small, good things to do every day!" With that, Thérèse said goodbye.

After Sister Saint Francis checked her work, Charlotte stuffed into her satchel the letter to her mother about her latest bad behavior. But happily, she folded the map inside a special copybook she kept for adventures.

Charlotte wanted to search for the garden the first chance she got. The first step would be to find the gardener, Monsieur Dubois. Since the map had the Bouchard's name on it, she would have to be careful. Charlotte remembered that a party was coming up at Louise Bouchard's house. If her mother still allowed her to go, that might be a good time to start.

Mysterious Lights and a Deer Path

∽ 4 ∽

At the Bouchard's party, Charlotte tapped her foot. Madame Bouchard, Louise's mother, had invited her daughter's classmates and all their mothers, including Charlotte's mother.

Louise and Charlotte had been competing with each other all of their lives. Who had the loopiest curls in her hair? Who got the highest grades? What made it worse was that Charlotte's mother pushed her to be friends with Louise. But her best friend was Anne.

Charlotte and Anne stared at a wiggly, orange fruit gelée.

"I can't wait for a bowl of that," Anne said.

"I'm whipping up something even better! I'll tell you soon. It's something fun. Just you wait."

"More fun than the chick in our classroom?"

"Yes, but my mother is still upset about that." In fact, Madame Masson, Charlotte's mother, was staring right at them. *How can I ever get away?* Charlotte looked right and left, searching for a chance to slip away. She wanted to find out more about the map and the Garden for Children.

Jean-Marc Dubois, the Bouchard's master gardener, had made the map. Could the garden be near Louise's house? *It's already evening. I have to move quickly. I have to create a distraction*, Charlotte thought. "I have an idea, Anne. Come with me."

Charlotte walked toward their young hostess who stood right at the center of the room. "Louise, why don't you sing us all a song? Your voice sounds like a songbird."

"Since when do *you* like my singing?" Louise raised an eyebrow, but she loved the spotlight. She twirled to show everyone the giant bow on her dress. "Will you sing after I do, Charlotte?" Louise came closer and whispered, "I bet I'm better."

Charlotte scrunched her face and whispered back, "Lucky for you, Louise, I have a sore throat."

Girls, and even Anne, pushed to the front. Everyone gathered around, even all the ladies. No one paid attention to Charlotte, so she made her move and edged toward the parlor's curtains.

In a garden, I won't have to compete with girls in singing or spelling, Charlotte thought. *An adventure is more fun anyway. When I find the garden, Anne and I can go there together! It will be our secret.*

Looking out into the early evening, she saw a light. Beyond the hedges and fence-like rows of flowers, where things were wild, it brightened, but then it disappeared.

Charlotte tiptoed to the next window. Like a beacon, the light had returned. She wondered if the light had anything to do with the garden. It *was* mysterious. And she *was* trying to find something hidden.

I'll have to go outside. It's not completely against the rules, since my mother is not far away. Charlotte stepped into the hallway. She'd never been in that part of Louise's house before. She tried one door, but it was locked. She tried another. It opened into a dusty, dark room.

Charlotte heard clanking pans and followed. A kitchen would have a door to the outside. *But what would the cooks think of a visiting girl wandering around?* She thought of her light-brown hair, the same color as Louise's. She thought of how Louise liked to dance all the time.

She saw a maid coming out of the kitchen with a large platter. She dashed under it and the maid spun. A cook rushed to help keep the food from falling. Charlotte pirouetted through the kitchen. "Good evening," she said, in what she hoped sounded like Louise's voice. She covered her face with dramatic arm motions and waltzed through the back door and onto the lawn. "I must dance in the starlight!" Charlotte exclaimed over her sholder. The servants were too busy to pay any attention.

Charlotte ran to the hedges. She didn't have a lantern, and the light from the house didn't reach that far. She tripped on a tree root and scuffed her boot.

Hearing footsteps, she scrunched down. *Hide!* she thought. *But where?*

5

Shivering, Charlotte hit the ground and rolled through cobwebs until she crashed under a bush. When she looked up, a spider dropped from the branches toward her eye.

As she started to shout, she saw a lantern heading straight toward her. She tried to stay still and quiet.

A blurry figure wearing a gardener's apron walked toward a group of small buildings. *It must be Jean-Marc Dubois.*

Charlotte tore away from the hedge and followed. Pale-yellow blossoms on trees looked down like eyes at her. On a peg sticking out from a cottage wall, she found a dark lantern, still warm. This must be where the gardener had gone inside. With the map held out in front of her, Charlotte knocked.

"*Bonsoir?*" the man with the gardening apron opened the door and asked. He looked about her grandfather's age, with a hawk face and sea-blue eyes. There were brown packets and leather gloves in his apron pockets

"*Bonsoir,* good evening, Monsieur," she answered. "Pardon me. Are you Monsieur Jean-Marc Dubois, the gardener of the Bouchard estate?"

"I'm not sure," the man said.

His answer was confusing. It seemed like he was being mysterious on purpose. What was he hiding?

A white, longhaired cat jumped next to him and started to purr. "Where did this cat come from?" the man asked.

"Well, the cat seems to know you," Charlotte said. As she reached to pet it, it tucked its flat face in a ball and slunk away from her. "Where is Jean-Marc Dubois?" Charlotte asked rather rudely. "Can you tell me? Do you know anything about this map?" She waved it at him.

The man looked at it. "A garden of fruit trees?"

A young maid, who was about twenty years old, approached. "What is going on here?" she asked. "Who are you?" To the gardener, she said, "That is *your* cat. Remember, Monsieur Dubois, you found him on a snowy night."

"So he *is* Monsieur Dubois! I am Charlotte Masson, a classmate of Louise Bouchard. I am here to ask about a map I found—a map of a hidden garden."

The maid pulled Charlotte aside. "Monsieur Dubois is forgetful. He is old now, and since his wife passed away, I've been helping him."

"Oh, I'm sorry. I didn't mean to upset him," Charlotte said.

The young maid grew less upset. Wearing a cheerful scarlet shirt and bonnet, she looked at Charlotte with round brown eyes. "My name is Elena," she said. "I came to work at the estate just last year. What is this about a map and a garden?"

Looking at the map, Charlotte thought of Thérèse and what she had said about small, good things. "I saw Monsieur Dubois wandering outside carrying a lantern. That doesn't seem safe," Charlotte said. "If I tried to find this garden, maybe it would help him. This map says that he's the one who planted it. If he could visit it, maybe he would remember things again. Will you let me look around? Chances are it's near the estate."

"I don't know what Monsieur Bouchard, the estate owner, might think," Elena said cautiously. Monsieur Bouchard was Louise's father.

"It's just a small thing—looking for a garden. We just need to cross the Bouchard estate to look on the other side. I'll start where I saw Monsieur Dubois wandering with the lantern."

Elena studied the map. "This *is* Monsieur Dubois' signature. I guess there would be nothing wrong with children playing in his garden. All right, I can watch over you when you're here."

Before she left, Charlotte saw some tea napkins on top of a washing basket.

"What are those?" Charlotte said, pointing to the napkins.

"Oh Monsieur Dubois' wife sewed them. That flower was special to them both," said Elena.

The map shows flowers near the entrance, Charlotte thought. *The flowers on the tea napkins might be important.*

After saying goodbye to Elena, Charlotte left and crept back inside to the party. There, everyone had gathered around Thérèse Martin. She must have arrived while Charlotte was talking to Monsieur Dubois and Elena. It was good that Thérèse didn't seem to have seen Charlotte slip in. Charlotte hoped that she and Thérèse might talk again.

Charlotte stepped to the corner of the room and took out her copybook for adventures. She wrote down a few clues. She drew where she had seen the lantern. She sketched the embroidered flowers. She made six pointed petals on a flower that looked like a star.

"Charlotte? Is that you?" Thérèse asked. "What are you working on?"

"I found a map to a Garden for Children in the library," Charlotte said. "I'm trying to find clues so that I can search for it!"

"That sounds like an exciting mission!" Thérèse looked around at the crowd. She whispered. "It reminds me of when my sister and I were in Rome visiting many interesting sights. We were supposed to follow a leader. Instead, we left our group and went down into a tomb. It was the grave of Saint Cecilia. She is one of my favorite saints. I took some of the dirt, but I probably wasn't supposed to. . . ." Just as Thérèse finished her sentence, some women came and led her away. She waved and smiled at Charlotte.

Thérèse sneaked away in Rome! Just like me. Charlotte couldn't believe it. Charlotte couldn't wait to tell Anne and search for the garden on their very next free day from school.

Will Anne and I really be able to find the Garden for Children? Charlotte wondered, *What will we find there?*

6

When the next free day from school came around, the warm sun was shining. The morning was so welcoming that a pond turtle had ventured up on a log to feel the sun's heat.

"This is the kind of day," said Charlotte, "for two girls to find a garden." On the walk over,

Charlotte had told Anne about the map and the gardener who couldn't remember making it. She thought they should start their search where she had seen the gardener with his lantern. Perhaps he had been searching for the garden?

The two girls walked toward the Bouchard house. It was the middle of March and the flowers made a kaleidoscope of colors.

The one cloud on this bright day was the possibility of running into Louise Bouchard. Sure enough, she saw them crossing the lawn.

"We're here to see Elena, the maid," Charlotte said.

"Your hat looks ridiculous," Louise shouted, poking her parasol at the sky.

"You know nothing about fashion or Paris," Charlotte said. To Anne, she said, "I've read all the fashion magazines. Feathers on hats are in fashion."

"Come on." Anne tugged Charlotte on their way.

"I don't have time to visit with either of you," said Louise. "I am busy with my dolls." She twirled her parasol as she spun away.

"I think Louise is lonely today. Do you?" Anne pulled on the strap of her hat under her chin and pushed down the ruffled flounces of her dress.

"She's not lonely. She has lots of friends in our class," Charlotte said. "But I'm not Louise's friend, and you shouldn't be either. You heard how she shrieked when that chick stepped on her copybook?"

"Yes, but…," Anne said.

"We are going to find the garden on our own," Charlotte said. "Just the two of us."

Anne and Charlotte found Elena and showed her the map again. They read, "Enter at the door near the flowers that are the color of dawn."

The maid shook her head and said, "There are flowers everywhere around here. How will you know when you've found the right ones?"

"Do you have any ideas?" Charlotte asked.

Elena bunched up her blue apron. "No. But maybe it's more fun if children find it. I don't have time to play anyway. I'll watch you though,"

The girls started searching by running every which way. All they did was run out of breath.

"Let's try to follow where the birds go," said Anne. "They might lead us to the flowers." That was difficult. A flock of sparrows settled under some orange tulips.

"Those orange flowers that look like cups, those could be the right flowers," Charlotte said. They didn't find a garden door nearby though.

Then a rabbit hopped over to a bunch of pink hyacinths. "My favorite flowers are those that look like a bunch of grapes," said Anne.

"What if the gardener has a favorite flower near the door?" said Charlotte.

Charlotte looked at her notes and pointed to the sketch of the embroidered flowers. "Maybe flowers in this shape are important. Madame Dubois, the gardener's wife, sewed these flowers on some tea napkins. They have six petals and look like a star."

"I know those flowers. They're lilies," Anne said.

"We also have to find 'flowers that are the color of dawn,'" Charlotte said. "What color is dawn?"

"Sunrise!" the girls exclaimed at once. They ran back to the orange tulips. They were the right color, but the wrong shape.

"So we're looking for flowers that are orange like these tulips, but star-shaped like lilies," Anne said. "Orange lilies."

The girls ran along the edge of the estate, around hedges, and through garden pathways. They searched everywhere for orange lilies. Charlotte was a fast runner, and Anne couldn't keep up.

Then, she saw it, a glimmer of bright orange. For once, Charlotte slowed down.

"Anne!" Charlotte shouted with excitement.

7

As Charlotte waited for Anne, a delicate shadow appeared before the small grove of orange lilies. "What's there? Who's there?" she whispered. A second slender shadow appeared, and a furry leg! Into the light, in front of the sunrise flowers, stepped a deer.

The deer's eyes shone like faraway moonlight. It dipped its head toward her, spun, and bounded through some saplings behind the orange flowers.

Charlotte's friendship with Anne was even stronger than her curiosity. She waited for Anne to catch up. "Anne, did you see the deer? These must be the lilies."

Beyond the flowers, the girls walked out onto a small meadow of breezy, green grass. Wildflowers grew in the meadow's furrows. In the taller grass, a mouse had woven a nest of crackly, brown fronds—a cozy bed for baby mice. At the end of the tiny meadow was a stone wall, and the girls could barely see the tall trees growing behind it.

At the center of the wall, there was a wooden door with an iron cross. Charlotte stepped to it and pushed, but something held it closed. "This must be the garden door. But how do we open it?"

The gardener had carved many shapes, like flowers and ivy, in the wood. Anne traced a curve on the right side. "Look at this carving. It could be a river."

"There's something else carved here in the middle of the ivy." Charlotte pointed to a wooden mother deer and its fawn.

"Do you think any of these are important?" Anne wondered aloud. "Wait, we're forgetting something . . ."

"The deer," the two girls said together.

"A *deer* led us here," said Charlotte. "Look at this mother deer and fawn."

As Charlotte traced her fingers over the outline, the carving moved. "It's a secret latch!" As she pushed it, the piece of wood tipped backward, and she saw a cord. "I think this cord must attach to the back of the door." She pulled on it and a hidden latch unhooked.

Anne softly tapped, and the door fell open. "Now only we know the way in. Well, the gardener used to, I suppose."

On the other side of the wall, a grove of leafy oak and beech trees rose high. "This looks just like the map!" Charlotte exclaimed.

The most surprising thing about this grove of trees was that a path of yellow primroses and dandelions led right through it.

"Elena, come see," Anne said. "Look! There's a yellow path on the map. We're inside the Garden for Children! Now we can look for the fruit trees."

"But the map doesn't show us where the fruit trees are," Charlotte said.

The two girls followed the yellow flower path. Elena waited at the entrance and worked on sewing. Everywhere the girls looked, they saw oak and beech trees, but no fruit trees. Brambly weeds had grown up among the tree trunks. They tried to walk off the flower path to look up into the trees for fruit or different leaves and branches between the oaks and beeches. But their dresses got caught and tangled in thorns. The girls decided it would be easier to follow the map's instructions after all and look for one of the four white stone paths.

They didn't walk very far when the yellow path ended at a ring of evergreens. The firs, heavy with green needles, stood like silent angels. They seemed to be waiting for the wind to blow so they could sing their prayers. The trees' branches hung so low that all the girls could see was more and more green.

Anne reached up to grasp one of the branches. As she pulled it down, she saw a wooden sign.

"Charlotte, come look," she called out. "There's a sign on this fir tree. Maybe it's a clue!"

8

Charlotte and Anne quickly ducked under the tree's low branches and grabbed the sticky, sap-covered trunk for balance. On the sign, under a white painted dove, someone had carved:

The Dove's Fruits in the Garden for Children

On the sign, four words made a circle: love, gentleness, joy, and patience.

The peaceful words and green trees filled Charlotte with calm—at first. "I'm not sure what it means," Charlotte said.

"I'm not either," Anne said. "Maybe you should write all of this down in your copybook."

"Good idea," Charlotte said. "The dove's fruit? Birds lay eggs; they don't grow fruit."

"Maybe it's fruit that doves like to eat . . . ," Anne said.

"But how could the dove eat joy . . . or love? That's a strange dove. Maybe it's imaginary and lives in a library."

"Maybe these are rules for the garden," Anne said.

"Oh, I hope not! I want to play in a place without rules," Charlotte said.

"These are nice rules, though. Joy, gentleness, love. . . . Being joyful is easy, right?" Anne said.

Charlotte frowned at the idea of rules. But she copied everything down, underlining "Dove's Fruits." As Charlotte was writing, a crow's call clattered out of the trees.

Charlotte shook off her surprise at the sudden noise. Then, when she looked down, she saw a small piece of blue knitted cloth on the ground. She picked it up. It was about the size of her hand and the shape of a small cape. "Anne, I think this is a cloak for a doll. It's lost."

An owl hooted.

"The time!" Anne exclaimed. "It's getting late."

❧

The next day after school, the two girls went with Charlotte's mother into town. After she stopped inside the post office, Charlotte heard running behind them.

"Olivier!" Charlotte shouted, smiling to her friend.

"Hello, Hello!" Olivier said, smiling back. "Out of the way, though!" He dashed in front and leaped onto a railing in front of the shops. As if on a tightrope, he ran on tiptoes. Vincent, Louise's older brother, ran after him.

Since he was chasing Olivier, Charlotte stuck out her foot and tripped him.

"You shouldn't have!" Anne exclaimed.

Vincent stumbled on the cobblestones, spun around, and made a face. He stomped off, shaking his fist at some laughing boys.

Olivier hopped off the railing. He took a bow near a donkey and a younger boy, his brother. Six-year-old Marc was washing a sign for the baker.

With a bouncy walk, Charlotte went over to the two boys as Anne followed.

"Hey, is that a chicken feather in your hat?" Olivier said. "I like it!"

Marc swirled some soapy water with the brush.

Charlotte started to turn red. "It should be fancier, but I haven't met any ostriches or peacocks. Only a chicken."

Staring at her hat, Marc flapped his arms like wings.

"Watch what the donkey's doing, Marc," Anne said.

"Meanwhile, I've torn my jacket again from that trick I just did," Olivier said. Olivier's and Marc's clothes had been patched up many times. Their parents didn't have enough money to make new jackets.

"The donkey!" Anne said.

The three of them turned around. The donkey had dipped its whole head in the soapy barrel.

"Get out of the water, you!" said Charlotte.

Olivier pulled on the reins. The donkey threw its head back and kicked the barrel over with its hoof. A foamy stream flowed down the street. Anne tried to set the barrel back up, but more water sloshed out.

"Hee-haw, hee-haw." With every haw, a huge bubble burst out of the donkey's mouth. Charlotte and Olivier dropped everything and laughed.

"Oh no!" Marc said. "The baker won't be happy. He won't give me coins." But the flour-covered shop owner came out to laugh, too. A wooden gargoyle seemed to smile from a perch of leaves carved on the next building.

After the donkey stopped making bubbles and noise, Anne asked Marc for his writing practice pages. She had given him the assignment the last time they had met. Olivier and Marc didn't always go to school. Their family needed money so much that the boys had to help by doing small jobs.

Sometimes Charlotte wished she could skip a day of school and wander around Lisieux with Olivier. She thought earning money sounded like an adventure. But Anne told her to be grateful for school and reminded her that the boys' lives were difficult.

As Anne examined a very neat "A," Charlotte watched her friends. She knew that they often had to move around. She thought about how the Garden for Children could be a safe place for Olivier and Marc to play in, too.

Charlotte thought of the stories she'd heard of the Martin family. Everyone knew that Thérèse, her sisters, and her father helped those who needed it. Charlotte didn't really want to pray all day, but she could still help people. She could share the garden with Olivier and his little brother. She decided to take them there—as soon as she could figure out more about the mission written on the map.

The First Tree

~ 9 ~

The next day, Charlotte was eager to look for the fruit trees and the doll that was missing her cloak. The Masson's maid dropped Charlotte off at the Bouchard estate to meet Elena and Anne.

"I know you don't like her, but shouldn't we ask Louise if she wants to play, too?" Anne said. Elena agreed and left to find her, but returned to tell them that Louise was in the middle of a waltz lesson.

Charlotte smiled. She didn't want Louise with them. She was still angry about being insulted. *Everyone knows that a chicken feather on a hat is fashionable. Everyone except Louise!* Charlotte thought.

Anne and Charlotte went to the edge of the Bouchard estate and then into the Garden for Children. Elena followed the girls and sometimes stopped to watch from a distance while mending some socks. Walking through the lily scent and along the yellow flower path, the girls soon came to the rings and rings of fir trees.

Charlotte reminded Anne of what they were setting out to do. "Our mission is to find the four hidden fruit trees. The first one should be apricot. Here is the map. Can you read what it says?"

Anne unfolded the map and began to read. "Follow four white stone paths, one for each tree. Careful! Ferns, leaves, and pine needles might have covered up the paths. On the stones, I've painted different kinds of fruit."

Then, Anne put her finger to her lips and pointed to a squirrel that had paused to look at the girls. Charlotte nodded and they tried to follow the skittering creature. It ran ahead to an old tree lit up by a ray of sunlight.

Both girls rushed to the tree. In the soft moss, they found a small wooden doll at the base of the trunk. The doll cradled in her arms a small baby with a halo.

The girls sat down on the ground and held the figure. Charlotte ran her fingers over grooved lines of brown hair. Rain and snow had softened the wood.

Solemnly, Anne fastened the blue cloak over a heart painted on the doll's dress. "I think she's Mary, the mother of Jesus."

"Why is she here?" Charlotte asked. "It's sad that she is alone in this garden. She needs someone to play with her, like us."

"Well, the gardener could have made the doll," Anne said.

"But we still haven't found any white stones," Charlotte said. "And this tree is another evergreen, not a fruit tree."

Charlotte lay on the needle-covered forest floor. "I feel something hard on my back." She turned over and started brushing needles aside. "It's a white stone! And another, and another! Anne, it's a stone path!" Anne leaned over to look.

"But this stone has a tiny heart painted on it— not a fruit," Anne observed.

"Still, it could lead us to a fruit tree . . . ," Charlotte said, standing up to charge forward. To mark the start of the path, Anne tucked the doll in the moss and followed.

Each stone in the path was not far from the one before. But the girls had to look for them under green moss or fallen pine needles.

Anne whispered the Hail Mary as she walked, while Charlotte led the way. The path ended with a circle of white stones, each with the same painted heart. In the center, stood a tree full of apricots.

"Magnificent!" the girls exclaimed. The orange fruit glowed like treasure.

"We don't even need a ladder!" Charlotte said.

After all the searching, the girls were hungry and ate a few apricots each. As they walked back toward the entrance of the garden, Anne put some apricots under the sign reading Dove's Fruits: joy, patience, gentleness, and love. "These are for squirrels that are too tired to climb."

As they walked home, Charlotte said, "Apricots—done. Clementines, little red fruits, and pears to go."

"It's great we found the tree," Anne said. "But I don't understand. The gardener said he painted a different kind of fruit on the stones. A heart isn't a fruit."

"Mysterious, isn't it?" Charlotte said.

What did it all mean?

~ *10* ~

On Sunday, while waiting for Mass, Charlotte thought the gold color in the stained-glass windows of the church looked like the yellow flowers in the Garden for Children. She was so happy she even smiled at her little brother, Theo.

"Trrrr, trrrr," Theo made a silly noise. "Trrrr, trrrr." He pointed to a clear window. Outside, a gray turtle dove with orange wings flew back and forth to a nest on a ledge. "I'm pretending to be a dove," he said.

Charlotte's and Theo's mother gave him a look. Charlotte knew that meant pretending and pointing were over. "That dove reminds us of the Holy Spirit, Theo. If we pray, the Holy Spirit will bring us his fruits. These are virtues, the good ways of behaving that you aren't showing right now!" said Madame Masson.

Her mother's words made Charlotte think carefully. *Now I understand! The dove in the garden is the Holy Spirit! The Holy Spirit has fruits that are virtues. Maybe the fruits in the Garden for Children are the fruits of the Holy Spirit. But how?*

She looked in her copybook. "Mama, are some of those fruits joy, patience, gentleness, and love?"

"Yes. Shh! Mass is about to begin," she answered with smiling eyes.

Elena and the gardener, Jean-Marc Dubois, were kneeling near the Martin family. As the priest led the Sign of the Cross, the gardener said the words and also made the Sign of the Cross. *He remembers the prayers*, Charlotte thought. *It's probably because he has said them so many times before.* Charlotte prayed carefully, too. After the Mass ended, Charlotte rushed to talk with Thérèse outside the church.

"What's going on with the garden you told me about?" Thérèse asked.

"My friend, Anne, and I have been having a real adventure. Our mission is to find four fruit trees." Charlotte pushed the garden map, which she always kept tucked in her copybook, toward Thérèse.

Thérèse looked at the map. "I'd love to visit."

"Really? That would be wonderful! Anne's been a big help though," said Charlotte. "Animals aren't afraid of her, and she notices everything."

"A true mission brings people who are different together as friends," Thérèse said. "You seem like you are very bold. That is important for an adventure."

"Thanks, but sometimes it gets me in trouble."
Charlotte frowned. Then, Theo ran in front, shouting "trrrr trrrr." The dove flew by in the sky. "Right now, my brother is the one getting in trouble, though." Thérèse laughed.

Charlotte's eyes lit up. "Anne and I have already found the apricot tree. It looked like the tree was full of gold! Sometimes, though, I wish we were searching for beautiful jewels, like rubies or emeralds, instead of just fruit."

"Someone might think apricots are worth more than jewels," Thérèse said. "Do you know someone who might need the food?"

Charlotte thought of Olivier. He and his family were always looking for ways to find food. She wanted to rush back to the garden that minute. "Yes, I do! One of my friends," Charlotte answered thoughtfully. Thérèse smiled.

As she thought of Olivier, Charlotte heard someone say, "The Bouchards will be cutting down fir trees to start a small forestry business."

What could that mean? Charlotte wondered. She remembered the tall fir trees in the garden.

Thérèse looked worried. "You must work to find all of the fruit trees quickly. You may not have much time."

Charlotte began to worry too, but then she saw Theo causing trouble. Chasing the dove, he crashed into Madame Bouchard. Wearing a heavy hat, she tumbled toward her daughter. Louise jumped out of the way—straight into a puddle. Muddy water sprayed everywhere.

"I think that poor dove just wants some peace," Thérèse said with a smile. "But your brother seems like he is having fun." Charlotte's mother grabbed Theo's hand and waved for Charlotte to come back so that the family could leave.

Charlotte knew that she had a new friend as she and Thérèse said goodbye.

Protectors of the Garden

~ 11 ~

Thick morning clouds hung low in the fog, as if they wanted to stay in the forest. But Charlotte and Anne hurried. They planned to meet Olivier near the Garden for Children and pick some sunny apricots for him to take home.

The boy had told them the day before that his mother was sick. She had coughed all night. When she woke up, her pillow was bright red from blood. Olivier's brother Marc and their baby sister were too young to understand. They still played beside their mother as if nothing had changed. But Olivier knew everything had. She was very ill.

Olivier had told Charlotte that he might have to leave his family in Lisieux to work in the big city of Rouen. That way, they could buy medicine. But when Charlotte told him about the fruit tree, Olivier's face lit up. "My mother loves apricots!" he had said.

Charlotte had thought and prayed about what Thérèse had told her. The garden's treasures might not be jewels, but something even more precious—something that would bring caring. Although Charlotte still hoped to find a glittering gem, she couldn't stop thinking about Olivier and his family.

As Charlotte prayed, she had an idea. *If we load Olivier's whole cart with apricots, maybe he could sell them,* Charlotte thought. *Then he would have enough money to buy medicine and still stay in Lisieux with his mother.*

When they entered the Bouchard's land, Charlotte heard footsteps and dogs barking. A man's sharp voice broke through the fog. "A short walk that way, there should be some fir trees, good for cutting down."

"There are fir trees in the Garden for Children." Charlotte said as she yanked her friend toward the voice.

"They'll see us," Anne said.

"Not in this fog. Besides, we need to find out what's going on," Charlotte whispered.

"But we told Olivier to meet us here. He can't find the garden by himself." Anne was right.

"There won't *be* a garden if they're planning to cut it down, Anne. Bend down low. No one will be looking for two girls in the fog." Charlotte was never one to back down from an adventure.

Staying as still as possible, the girls watched. They could make out the shapes of four men. One stood in front, pointing a rifle toward a row of flowers. He jabbed his hand toward the Garden for Children. The three others wore workman's caps. They all held sharp saws and axes. Two hounds on leashes lunged at the swirling fog.

"That's Louise's father, Monsieur Bouchard," Charlotte said. "Why does he have a gun? Are they afraid of dandelions? Or trees?"

Monsieur Bouchard said, "These trees have grown a long time. They are good for firewood and furniture. The lumber will bring in some new money for the estate. This way. These directions are old and not very clear. My gardener wasn't that careful."

"Isn't that line marked 'Dubois'?" one of the men asked.

"I don't see a line," Louise's father said sharply. He turned the men toward the children's garden.

Charlotte didn't understand what they were talking about, but she knew where they were walking. She balled up her fists.

"They'll trample the path," Anne said. "They'll knock over the Mary doll!"

"They may even cut down the apricot tree," Charlotte said. "But now we really need it for Olivier's mother!"

As the girls whirled about, not sure what to do, fog cloaked the lilies at the garden's entrance.

"We can't see a thing," the men said. They peered all around them in the dim gray light.

All of a sudden, the deer of the garden sprang across the open field. She moved away from the lilies and the safety of the wall and toward the house's formal gardens. She bounded over a hedge. The dogs ripped free and rushed after her.

Anne pointed to the trailing leashes. Hidden in fog, Charlotte dove after them but missed.

"The dogs!" The confused men scattered.

"Grab those hounds!" shouted Louise's father.

"They must not catch the sweet deer!" Charlotte whispered.

～ 12 ～

Charlotte's heart beat fast as the hounds jumped the hedge with room to spare.

"Keep out of sight," she whispered. Anne and Charlotte ran behind some bushes to see what had happened. "What if the dogs are tearing into the deer?"

Instead, the two dogs spun around Olivier and wagged their tails happily. He gave them little treats from his jacket and patted their backs. "Hide," he told them as he waved with his hands.

The girls ducked behind a hedge.

"Boy!" The men came into the Bouchard's formal garden. "What are you doing here? This is private property. Street children aren't allowed!"

Olivier lowered his eyes and took off his cap. "I'm sorry. I'm rounding up these dogs. They seemed a little lost." He picked up the leashes. "Here you are."

Louise's father pushed in front. "Thank you for gathering my dogs. They are worth a lot. But now, get off my land."

"Yes, Monsieur," Olivier said.

Monsieur Bouchard turned to the men and said, "We'll try this again when the weather clears up."

Olivier walked away, stepped behind a tree, and climbed right up. He disappeared into the misty leaves. The girls slipped from their hiding place and huddled under the same tree.

"We should try to get the apricots another day," Anne said softly. "We're already sneaking around, and I'm really scared we'll get caught."

"No," Charlotte said. "You saw them. They can't even handle a bit of fog. Now is the best time. They're leaving. You did all right with the dogs, Olivier. But you were *supposed* to bring a cart. How are we going to carry all the apricots?"

Olivier flipped upside down. "Nothing impresses you, Charlotte." He somersaulted off, caught a lower branch, and jumped to the ground. "I've hidden it under a bush of some stinky flowers. Now I smell like a rose. All the other boys are going to tease me."

"I'm worried about taking the apricots," Anne said.

"Are you sure this is all right?" Olivier asked.

"Well, the gardener who planted the tree is very old and doesn't remember anything," Charlotte explained. "But the map says that he made the whole garden for children. It's his garden and we're children. So I think that everything in it is for us."

"We have to pass through the Bouchard's land to get there. That's the sneaky part," Anne said.

"But we need to." Charlotte paused. "We're sorry about your mother, Olivier."

Olivier stood silently. He wiped his face with his sleeve. Charlotte saw a flower he'd picked tucked in his jacket. *For his mother*, she thought.

The three friends went to the cottage to find Elena. "Hide behind these trees, Olivier," Charlotte warned. "She might think my mother wouldn't want us all playing together. It's best if she doesn't see you." Many families only allowed their children to play with others who had the same amount of money. Charlotte didn't like that way of thinking.

"Still, I'd love to see the garden," Olivier said.

Charlotte knocked on the cottage door like a hammering woodpecker.

"Who is this?" came Elena's voice from behind them. She had walked from the main house right into the hiding boy.

13

"Sorry," said Olivier, "I . . . I am here to—"

"Make a delivery," Charlotte interrupted.

"Come on. Tell me the truth." Elena put her hands on her hips.

"He is our friend," Charlotte said. "He is here to get some apricots for his mother who is sick. His name is Olivier Bernard."

Elena's eyes widened. "Bernard? I know that family. Once when I was younger, we had no gifts for Christmas. Charles Bernard carved us little farm animals out of wood. His wife knitted toy blankets for them. You're their son? You look like your father."

"Yes, that's my family," Olivier answered with pride.

"Don't worry. You can all go to the garden together," Elena said.

After thanking Elena, they all walked to the garden. Inside, they headed straight to the Mary doll. "Hail Mary," both girls said.

Olivier stood back a little way. "Is that doll supposed to be Mary? Do you think she really listens to prayers?"

"The doll can't hear anything, but Mary does. She can help you by telling your prayer to Jesus," Charlotte said. "That's how it works."

Olivier sat down by the doll and whispered something. Elena reminded him to make the Sign of the Cross at the end. They said together, "In the name of the Father, and of the Son, and of the Holy Spirit."

Saying the prayer reminded Charlotte of her brother and the dove at the church.

"Anne!" Charlotte said with excitement. "I forgot to tell you. I figured out what the dove is— the one on the sign here in the garden. It's the Holy Spirit!"

"Why didn't I think of that?" said Anne. "The Holy Spirit is always with us. But what about the words on the sign? Gentleness . . . joy . . . patience . . . love."

"They are some of the fruits of the Holy Spirit," Charlotte said. "They are gifts from God. They make us good like he is." Charlotte was trying to remember them all, but Olivier interrupted.

"What do we do next? How do we find the apricots?" Olivier asked.

"We follow these white stones." Charlotte pointed to the ground.

The three friends walked to the apricot tree and loaded the cart. "It's like a whole pirate's chest full of treasure," Olivier said. "They're ripe for so early in the year. Apricots are my mother's favorite."

Charlotte spun around. *It was just like Thérèse had said.* The apricots did feel more precious than jewels. Charlotte felt like a bird flying for the first time. Olivier was her friend, but she hadn't known him that well before. Now that she had helped him, she knew him better.

Charlotte and Anne told Olivier more about the mission to find the four fruit trees.

"On the stones, the gardener painted different kinds of fruit. There were hearts on the path to the apricot tree," Anne added.

As the cart's wheels bumped along the white stones on the way out, Olivier skipped and chatted. "I don't know how a heart can be a fruit. Where are we going to find the next stone path?"

Charlotte thought about Olivier's question.

A light rain began to fall, and Elena told the children they should head home.

As they left the garden, a noise came from Louise's house. *Hadn't all the window shutters been closed before?* At one window under its own little gable roof, the shutter slats were open. Someone could have seen Olivier with his cart.

Charlotte knew in her heart that the apricots had come from the Garden for Children, and Olivier's sick mother needed them. Still, she felt uneasy.

The Second Tree

~ 14 ~

A few days later, Charlotte and Elena headed to the Carmel of Lisieux. Elena had agreed to go with Charlotte on her day off. They both wanted to see where Thérèse would spend the rest of her life.

After a short walk, they came to an iron fence. A building rose up, but statues of Mary and saints seemed to welcome everyone.

Elena said, "I've heard that there are gardens inside, a chapel, a kitchen, and many bedrooms."

"Many places for Thérèse to pray. She'll like that," Charlotte said.

A dusty, brown sparrow balanced on the fence before hopping off. It landed at Elena's feet, then sprang up to the sky. "Look at the tiny sparrow," Charlotte said. "It can fly away to Paris any time it likes. But Thérèse won't be able to leave once she comes here. Why would anyone *want* to do that?" Charlotte's cheeks turned pink. She wished she had just kept quiet.

"I don't know," Elena answered softly. "But maybe she believes that it's what Jesus wants her to do."

"Thérèse told me that it's enough to do small things for God. Staying behind a wall and praying for the rest of your life doesn't seem small to me."

Returning from Carmel, Charlotte asked Elena if they could walk faster to meet Anne. Charlotte and Anne had agreed that they would look for the second tree that afternoon.

When they turned a corner, they ran right into Louise. Her hat was so big it almost blocked the entire sun. Charlotte thought that the expression on Louise's face looked like she'd just stepped on a slug.

"Where do you think you're going?" Louise asked.

Charlotte couldn't think of anything to say. She didn't want to tell the truth.

"Elena, will you take me where they are going?" Louise jutted her chin out.

"I think Charlotte," Elena said, "should explain." As Anne walked up to the group, Elena added, "Anne, you can make sure Charlotte doesn't leave anything out."

Charlotte scrunched up her face. She knew that Elena, who worked for Louise's family, would tell the whole truth.

Charlotte tried to rush through the story. "I found a map with Gardener Dubois' name on it. I talked to him about it, so I'm the leader. It says we need to find four hidden fruit trees to complete the mission—"

"Well, if you have a map, just follow it to find the trees!" Louise said with her hands on her hips.

"If you'd stop interrupting, Louise, you'll find out why it's not that easy!" Charlotte paused and then went on. "The trees aren't on the map. We have to find white stone paths to the trees. Anne and I have been looking for them. But the map warns us to be careful. It says that pine needles and leaves could be covering up the paths."

"But wouldn't it be easier to find the trees than the stone paths?" Louise asked.

"We thought of that, too," Charlotte said. "But there are lots and lots of trees."

"We have found one of the paths already," Anne said. "It went to an apricot tree. The gardener painted different kinds of fruit on the path stones."

"Different kinds of fruit?" Louise asked. "You mean he painted apricots to lead to the apricot tree?"

Anne answered, "No. He painted *hearts* to lead to the apricot tree."

"Hearts? Hearts aren't a kind of fruit. That's strange!" Louise said.

"Well, I suppose that's what makes it mysterious," Elena said.

"I guess I'll go along." Louise sighed. "You should have told me about this earlier, you know!"

As they walked to the garden, Charlotte strode in front, kicking a rock ahead of her. *Why do we have to bring her along?* Then, Charlotte remembered. *Louise hasn't seen that the fourth tree is marked "treasure." I still think it could be a jewel. At least she doesn't know anything about that.*

When they got to the door, Charlotte blocked the latch. "I'm not going to show her *all* the secrets," Charlotte whispered to Anne. "Especially since Louise is so ungrateful!"

∽ 15 ∽

Anne and Charlotte led Louise past the apricot tree where Anne saw a small, gray bird gathering moss for a nest.

"Why don't we follow the bird?" asked Anne. "A squirrel helped us find a doll, which we think the gardener made. Near there we found the first path." She dashed off as the bird flew. The other two girls shrugged and followed. Even Elena walked quickly. Above a circle of ferns, the bird disappeared. Louise pranced ahead and danced a waltz step.

"Such a show-off," Charlotte muttered.

"There's rustling over there. Maybe it's our bird," Anne said.

"I'll take a look," Charlotte said. She brushed past Louise, who was near a tall oak tree ahead. "Well, there is a wooden peg on the trunk. But there's nothing hanging from it. Like Anne said, last time, we found a doll near the white stone path. So if there was something hanging from here, we might be near a new path."

Anne started to look for white stones around the tree. But everywhere she looked, there was Louise— her giant skirt covering the ground!

"Hey!" Charlotte said. "Why do you keep blocking her way? What are you hiding?"

Anne held Charlotte's arm. "Charlotte, that's not nice."

"I'm just standing in the ferns," Louise defended herself, "just like the two of you."

"Then let me look where you're standing! Step aside." Louise did, spinning her back away from Charlotte, who scrambled and dug under the sword-shaped plants.

Turning red, Charlotte said, "No stones under here. Wait, what's behind your back? Did *you* take something off the wooden peg?"

"Really, Charlotte," Anne said, "Louise wouldn't hide anything from us."

Charlotte craned her head around. Louise spun again so her back faced Anne.

"Wait! She *does* have something in her hand," Anne said.

"I told you we couldn't trust her." Charlotte turned to Louise. "Hand it over!"

"I'll *show* it to you," Louise said, "but I'm not handing it over." She lifted up a nest box. "Monsieur Dubois was the gardener for *my* family. When he made this garden for children, he was thinking of my brother and me. *I'm* the one who is supposed to find the fruit trees, not you, Charlotte Masson."

"The map doesn't say 'Garden for Louise.' It says 'Garden for Children'!" Charlotte argued.

"Be careful," warned Anne. "That's a nest box! There may already be eggs inside. They'll break!"

"I'll hand it over to *you*, Anne, but not to Charlotte." Louise shoved one hand out to block Charlotte and held out the box to Anne.

Anne peered in, shaking. "Good. I don't see any eggs. Only moss and grass." Holding the box as if it were a fragile shell, she hung it back on the peg.

"Well, any eggs that were there could have fallen out with all this," said Charlotte. "Get out of the way, Louise! I have to find the white stone path."

Elena tried to calm things down. "Charlotte, you can't keep Louise from joining in. As you just said, this garden is for *all* children. Everyone is allowed to look for the trees."

Charlotte huffed. Louise put her nose in the air. Anne paused and thought. Then, all three of them began to search again.

Anne followed a line of dandelions down a small ridge. "I found an egg painted on a white stone!"

"What do painted eggs on rocks have to do with fruits?" Louise's voice was loud enough to wake up every sleeping animal in the forest. "I don't see how that could be a different kind of fruit, like the map says."

"But we found the apricot tree at the end of a path of white stones," Charlotte said. "*You* couldn't find an orchard tree if fruit fell on your head!"

The girls looked all around the little dandelion meadow. But the stone with an egg painted on it seemed to be the only one.

Except . . . Charlotte saw a log that had fallen, stuck lengthwise above the ground like a fence. Waist-high and surrounded by trees, it blocked her way. *I could try to crawl under, in yucky mud in a ditch. Or, I could go over,* she thought.

When Anne and Louise weren't looking, Charlotte ran straight toward the log, closer and closer. She jumped and her stomach ended up flopping flat on the log. Her head went upside down, her flegs flew over, and she somersaulted. *Thwack.*

Charlotte didn't land on her feet, but it didn't matter since she saw a second white stone. The third stone she spotted turned out to be a slimy mushroom. But then, she found more real stones, and, at last, a glimmer of orange fruit!

"What's beyond this fallen log?" Louise called out as Elena looked on.

"*I've* found the tree. I'm the champion!" Charlotte shouted. "You have to go over or under that fallen log!"

The hidden, colorful tree stood in a sunny grove hugged by many beech and oak trees. It was bright and full of the last clementines of the season.

As Anne and Louise made their way over the log, Charlotte thought, *I wish we didn't have to share this tree with Louise. Maybe she'll leave us alone after today.*

The girls picked as many clementines as they could carry and ate them on the way out of the garden. Charlotte looked toward the tree with the sign of the Holy Spirit Dove's Fruits. She thought of the four words there: joy, patience, gentleness, and love. *I didn't show any of those today,* she thought sadly. *Especially not gentleness. I hope there really weren't any eggs in the nest box. They would certainly have broken.*

The Third Tree

❦ 16 ❦

Later that week, Charlotte, Anne, Elena, Olivier, and his little brother Marc all set out to the garden in search of the third fruit tree. *No Louise this time! What a relief,* Charlotte thought.

"I like your new purse." Anne pointed to Charlotte's dark velvet bag trimmed with stars.

"Thanks. My brother, Theo, took one of the stars, though, and ran off with it. He's always in trouble. I would have brought him today, but my mother said no. He got in trouble at school. Anyway, I made the purse last night after I spent time staring at my copybook. I went over all that I had written about the garden, especially the Dove's Fruits," said Charlotte.

"Yes, the fruits of the Holy Spirit," said Anne.

Elena grabbed the girls' arms. "Look ahead." Two men came crashing through the ferns in the distance. Olivier ducked down into the forest with Marc.

"I'm afraid that they're woodcutters for Monsieur Bouchard!" Elena said.

"I'm going to try something to get them out of here," Charlotte said.

Charlotte stood right in front of the men. "What are *you* doing here? This is *my* garden."

"Mademoiselle Bouchard?" The men thought Charlotte was Louise, the daughter of Monsieur Bouchard.

"Axes are not allowed here. Shouldn't you be fixing the barn door? My pony almost escaped!" Charlotte made up a story.

"But Monsieur Bouchard told us . . . ," one man started to say.

"My father and I talked about the barn door this morning! It's more important than this."

The other man said, "We had better head over to the barn and check."

Charlotte breathed out a sigh in relief and turned to Elena. "At least they have never met Louise. I don't want to get you in trouble though."

"I don't know what to do," Elena said.

"We can't let them cut down trees. We can't let them destroy what the gardener has made," Charlotte said.

"Are you crazy?" Olivier came up from the ferns with his little brother. "What's going to happen when they figure out you aren't Louise?"

"You look a little like her . . . but not that much," Anne said.

"I'm sure they've never seen her up close." Charlotte nodded her head. But she started not to feel so brave. And she knew she'd told a lie. It reminded her of the chick and all the trouble she'd caused. Even if it had been for a good reason, it was still wrong. But Thérèse had said Jesus understood when people made mistakes.

"Pretending to be Louise got rid of the wood-cutters for now," said Elena. "But we have to try to talk to the Bouchards about protecting the garden. But how can I? I'm just a maid."

Charlotte tried to act sure of herself. She marched ahead without looking again at Elena's worried face.

When they got to the nest box, Charlotte gave orders: "Marc, you stay with Olivier. We are looking for a white stone path that leads to the third tree."

Charlotte liked exploring in the forest. But after passing mossy trunk after mossy trunk, she became discouraged. Where was the next path?

"Hey, over here!" she could hear the distant shout of Olivier.

Charlotte almost ran into Anne as they arrived where the boys were.

"Look!" said Olivier with his arms up as if he'd won an award.

"I want to go on it!" Marc exclaimed.

"Go on what? I don't see a thing," Charlotte said.

"Look up," Olivier said.

The girls looked up as high as they could until they saw what Olivier and Marc were talking about.

"Wow," exclaimed Charlotte.

"I've found something happy and wonderful!" Olivier grinned.

The slats of a ladder were nailed to the trunk of a nearby tree. At the top was a wooden platform. Above the platform there was a beam that connected to another tree. In the middle of the beam, a swing was hanging, but not the kind of swing they were used to seeing. This one was ten feet off the ground.

"That *is* fun and happy, right?" Olivier said again.

"No, I think *that* is scary," said Anne.

"This swing could be dangerous," Elena said. "I'll stand underneath to catch anyone who falls."

"It looks crooked," said Anne as she shifted one side to the other. "I don't want to go!"

"Scared as a wet hen!" said Charlotte.

"That's not nice! I helped you get a chick out of our classroom, remember?" Anne said.

"I want to go first," said Charlotte.

"No, I do," argued Olivier.

The children drew twigs to decide the order. Olivier won. Anne smiled when she wasn't first.

"I can pretend to fly through the forest," said Olivier, preparing to climb.

"I don't even need the ladder." Olivier was on the platform in seconds. He jumped on the swing with force and threw his head back. His cap flew down, landing on a branch. "I feel like a falcon. It's great! I'm taller than some of the trees!"

Soon it was Charlotte's turn. She was shaking as she went up the ladder. She shrugged and tried to act calm. The ground beneath her seemed a long way down.

"Just hop out," said Olivier.

"I know what I'm doing," Charlotte said. She grabbed the rope of the swing and hopped. For a second, she almost missed.

Charlotte heard the breeze in the firs. *Do small things for God*, she remembered Thérèse saying. *Thank you God, for this beautiful garden that my friends and I can play in*, she thought.

The first swing backward was the scariest—and most fun. Charlotte went higher and higher, and then was pulled back to the comfort of the forest and her friends. Every time she flew forward, she felt as if she were flying with a flock of invisible birds.

Next, Anne went up each ladder step as if she were taking a test. But after, she said, "I went as fast as squirrels jumping from tree to tree."

Olivier yelled to Marc, "Come on, we can go together!"

Olivier took his little brother on the swing. They had to go slowly to be safe, but they both were laughing with delight.

When they were back on the ground, Olivier said, "Taking my brother on the swing was my good deed for the day!"

Charlotte stared at him for a moment. She hadn't told him Thérèse's prayer that all of Charlotte's friends would find small, good things to do every day.

But Charlotte was soon knocked back to earth.

17

"We should invite Louise," Elena said. "She would love the daring swing, just like you do, Charlotte."

"I know," said Charlotte, "but Louise and I aren't friends. She got to see the clementine tree. That's enough."

"This swing is even better. You should invite her," said Elena.

"Elena's right, Charlotte," said Anne.

There was a long pause. "But Elena, we haven't even found the third tree," Charlotte said. "Let's look for stones to lead the way."

Charlotte tried to ignore the look of disappointment on Elena's face. She turned and pointed to a white rock not far away. Anne pointed to Marc.

Marc looked around slowly. "I see it!" Marc said. "I see it. Right next to Anne's foot. It has a sun painted on it!"

"Can you find the next one? We'll follow you." Charlotte smiled, and Marc jumped from one stone to the next.

"Hopping is happy," said Marc.

The sun reminded Charlotte of how happy she felt reaching for the sky. "Olivier, what did you say again when you first found the swing?"

"That I found something happy," Olivier answered.

"Joy," Charlotte said. She remembered something important. She opened her copybook. "Everyone listen again to the Dove's Fruits from the wooden sign: love, gentleness, joy, and patience."

"The sun makes me think of joy," Olivier said. "I'm happier on sunny days. Marc and I don't have to stand on the street in the rain." He jumped up and down. "I think the sun is joy. It's a fruit, a dove's fruit."

Charlotte nodded so much her hat almost fell off. "The sun is a different kind of fruit, a fruit of the Holy Spirit: joy." She grabbed her best friend. "What do you think, Anne?"

"I think we need to match the hearts we found for the apricot tree. And we need to match the eggs we found for the clementine tree," said Anne. She looked inside the copybook. "We need to match them with gentleness, love, or patience."

Anne thought aloud, "I believe eggs are gentleness. Parent birds must treat the shells gently or they'll break. The baby birds will die."

"I know the hearts that took us to the apricot tree are love." Charlotte opened and lifted her arms in a big heart. "Olivier, you found help for your mother there."

"Yes, I believe that path is love," Olivier said. "So, patience is left."

"What's patience?" Marc asked.

"Waiting without complaining," Elena answered.

Olivier lifted his brother up and spun him. "You are always patient. You were last to go on the swing, and you didn't get upset at all."

As soon as Marc was back on the ground, he went back to hopping on suns. At the end, though, they came to a shrub without fruit.

"I thought we were supposed to find a tree. This isn't much taller than I am," Olivier said.

"Wait," Anne said. "I've seen this in my grand-mother's garden. It's a red currant shrub. Isn't that what the map says? See, it has five-sided blossoms. In summer, the plant will pop out in all sorts of red berries like fireworks at a celebration."

The friends stayed beside the red currant shrub to play. As Anne sketched a flower and the boys ran around, Charlotte pulled up some weeds from around the plant. The deer of the garden watched them from behind some oaks. *This peaceful moment will always remain in my memory*, Charlotte thought.

On the way home, Olivier turned a cartwheel on the open lawn of the Bouchard estate. Charlotte grabbed the back of his jacket. "Stay closer to the hedge. Someone might see you."

"Oh no! I forgot my cap," Olivier stopped short.

"We'll get it next time," Charlotte said, "We need to keep going now."

Anne held up one of the red currant blossoms like a flag. Charlotte pulled her arm down. "Don't make such a show!"

The shutters on the second-floor window of Louise's house opened a little bit and closed again. Charlotte shivered even though the sun was warm. *Is Louise watching?* Charlotte worried. *She will be angry if she finds out about the swing.*

A Friend in Trouble

~ 18 ~

A few days later, Charlotte and her mother went to the bakery to pick up a baguette loaf of bread and to do other errands. As they left the bakery, Charlotte was daydreaming about the garden when she almost tripped over an overturned cart.

She stopped when she saw the small, painted, green frog on the handle of the cart. This was Olivier's cart.

A bad feeling came over her. Charlotte lifted the cart up and stood it on all four wheels. *Strange he'd leave it this way*, she thought. A clementine, left behind, rolled in the dust. Something had to be wrong. Olivier wouldn't have left things like that behind. She whipped her head around searching for him. Her friend was nowhere to be seen.

Then, Charlotte saw that she was in front of the jail. "Mama, may I please stay here for a moment?"

"All right. I'll be at the butcher's shop. Don't be long," her mother said.

Charlotte rushed to the large, gray door of the jail and courthouse. She pushed against it and knocked on it until her hands turned red.

She ran to the side of the building. "Olivier?" she called out.

A boy's hand was wrapped around the bars of a window. "Charlotte?" said a shaky voice.

The window was so high that Charlotte could barely hear him. She climbed a nearby tree.

"Olivier!"

"Get down from the window, boy!" a man's voice said. "People are trying to sleep in this cell!"

"What happened? Why are you in jail?" Charlotte said.

"I was in the garden. . . . They said I was steal-ing. . . . I told Marc to run back and hide, near joy, near the swing. I told him to wait for me there."

"I'll need to get your parents," Charlotte said.

"No! No! Not Mama. She's too sick," Olivier exclaimed. "And my father is working in another town today."

"But you *weren't* stealing! It's a garden for children. Who said you were stealing?" she asked.

"The workers, the ones with the dogs. They got the police inspector," Olivier said.

"The workers for the Bouchards? Louise's family?" Charlotte asked.

"I don't know," Olivier said. The sound of heavy footsteps came from inside. "Take this nice frog I found, Charlotte. Protect it. . . ." Olivier pushed the green animal out in the space toward her and dropped his hands away from the bar.

Not sure what to do, Charlotte put the frog in the velvet purse she'd made. She gripped the branches of the tree and climbed down. *This can't be happening.*

"I don't know what to do!" she cried, then prayed silently, *Jesus, show me what to do! Maybe if I get the map*, she thought, *I can show the inspector that the garden is for children. That it's all right for children to go there.* Charlotte looked at the stone building. She couldn't be sure that anyone would listen to her. *Would the police even open the door?* she wondered.

Charlotte ran across the street and found her mother. "I have to run home."

"Why, Charlotte? What's going on?" her mother asked with concern.

"I need to help my friend." Charlotte held back tears.

"Which one?" her mother asked.

"Olivier . . ."

"Charlotte," her mother said, "it is fine to be kind to him and give him charity. But I prefer that you play with Louise or Anne."

"I'm sorry, Mama. I really need to do this. I don't have time to explain."

Before Madame Masson could stop her, Charlotte turned to race down the street.

Charlotte didn't want to leave her mother without saying more, but there was no time.

Charlotte ran to her house. When she opened the door, her cat dashed past her, his fur puffed up.

Why is he scared? The sky, it's gray, she thought. The leaves of the trees whipped. They looked silver in the dimming light. A storm was coming.

Skipping every other step, she sprang up the stairs. Charlotte grabbed the map to the garden and then found her little brother, Theo, pulling the strings of a marionette puppet. She scribbled a note to Anne asking her to look for Thérèse. Older and wiser, Thérèse would know how to help. "Theo, run to Anne's house and give her this note."

"It's going to rain, Charlotte. Mama told me to stay here."

"Please. You have to. My friend is in jail, and his little brother is hiding in a forest garden. I must find him before the storm. Please, Theo, Anne's house isn't far. I'm asking her to find Thérèse!"

"Yes, then, I'll go." They set off in opposite directions.

~ 19 ~

Charlotte ran toward the jail under graying clouds. Bits of paper and dust lay scattered down the street. Everything seemed to be out of place.

As she arrived, she could see the Bouchard family's carriage stopped outside. *Louise had probably seen Olivier and told her father! It was all her fault!* Charlotte went over to the carriage and yanked back the curtain. Louise was inside.

"Louise!" Charlotte shouted. "I need to get into the courthouse. Is your Papa in there? My friend, Olivier, he wasn't stealing!"

Louise put a doll from her lap on the seat next to her. Beside it was Olivier's cap! Her eyes looked red.

"I can't help. My father said that a troublemaker was stealing fruit from our land."

"Olivier isn't a troublemaker!" Charlotte said. "Besides, how did your father know that Olivier was in the garden? You went back to the garden by yourself, didn't you? You found Olivier's cap near the swing. You've been watching us, haven't you, Louise? And you told your father about Olivier! Why would you do that?"

Tears appeared in Louise's eyes. She looked down. "I did tell my father about the boy. But I didn't mean for him to get the police."

"Well now Olivier is in jail!" Charlotte cried. "He's my friend."

"Olivier? Is that his name? Why did you take a street boy like him to the garden? What about your classmates—like me? Shouldn't you have invited us?"

"I suppose so . . ." Charlotte felt a bit sorry. She didn't want to look Louise in the face, but she had to keep going. "I did leave you out, and I am sorry. I've been hiding a lot of things from you. I suppose I should have told you about the garden when I told Anne."

"I saw all of you. You found the swing without me." It was clear that Louise was more sad than angry.

"I promise we'll take you with us the next chance we get and show you everything," Charlotte pledged. Louise looked straight at Charlotte and smiled.

"I really didn't mean to get Olivier into this much trouble," she said. "But my father is so angry. I don't know how I can help."

"Help me get into the courthouse by calling out to your father," Charlotte pleaded.

Charlotte felt a hand grip her shoulder. "What is going on?" Madame Masson asked.

"I'm sorry for running off, but I've got to get into the courthouse to help Olivier. He's been locked up, and it's not fair."

"Young girls from good families do not go to courthouses or talk to the police. You'll get into trouble, Charlotte!"

What if her mother was right? Would she be put in jail, too? But hadn't Thérèse told her to be bold? It was a garden for *all* children. Olivier hadn't done anything wrong.

"Did you hear me?" Charlotte's mother asked.

Charlotte spoke again. "Even though I'm small, Mama, I can help. That's what Thérèse Martin has been teaching me. I know you want me to be polite and quiet. But sometimes doing the right thing is

disruptive! Olivier's mother is sick. The fruit was for her to eat. It was also for Olivier to sell. Then his family was able to buy medicine for her. This isn't fair!"

Madame Masson was silent for a moment. She placed her hands in prayer. "I didn't know that he was trying to help his sick mother. Charlotte, you're right. You *must* try to do something about it."

Charlotte took Louise's hand. The girls walked up the steps together to the jail. Charlotte's mother followed, putting a shawl around Charlotte as the cold wind blew. Louise called out for her father and, after a few moments, the inspector opened the heavy, gray door.

"You shouldn't be interrupting," Louise's father said. "This is no place for a well-born girl like yourself." Louise was silent.

Charlotte shoved in front of her. "Inspector Dufour!"

20

Charlotte trembled as everyone in the room turned to look at her.

"You are an excellent inspector. But this is a terrible mistake. My name is Charlotte Masson. My friend, Olivier Bernard, wasn't stealing fruit. He was picking fruit from a garden that is for children."

Louise's father turned toward her and shook his finger. "Surely, this girl isn't one of your friends."

Louise stepped back.

Inspector Dufour said, "Monsieur Bouchard, are you sure that the boy really was on your land?"

"Yes, my daughter told me that the boy was in my grove, picking clementines. It's on my estate as the land records show. If I have to have my clerk bring over all the papers, I will. You've seen this boy. He's a street boy."

Land records? I don't understand what they are talking about, Charlotte thought. But she had to be strong for Olivier.

"Olivier's mother is sick," Charlotte said. "That is why he was in the Garden for Children. He wanted to help her."

"Now young lady," the inspector said, "you seem to have a soft heart, but a loud voice. It's kind that you care about this family, but all that matters is who owns the land. It is clear that the boy does not."

Charlotte felt someone's hand slip into hers. It was Thérèse, who whispered, "You're so brave."

Charlotte turned to see Anne standing behind her as well.

Charlotte took a deep breath and began to feel stronger. "But the garden belongs to the Bouchard's gardener, Monsieur Dubois. He planted the garden *for children*."

"Then, we should bring the gardener here to tell us about it," the inspector said.

"He is old and has lost his memory. I have a map here, though, that shows that he made his garden for children." Charlotte stretched the map to the tall inspector's face.

Louise's father rubbed his chin. "It's true that I gave Monsieur Dubois some land on my estate. It was just a small, wild grove of pines. I thought he could cut down the firs and sell them. Then he wouldn't have to worry about money. But this shows fruit. I didn't give him any fruit trees."

The inspector looked. "I see a scribbled picture, not a map."

Charlotte's legs shook. *Maybe it wasn't a map, after all?* She thought if she showed the map, the inspector would set Olivier free. But he hadn't. She didn't know what to do. She turned toward her friends.

Thérèse grasped Charlotte's and Louise's hands. Her lips moved silently.

Charlotte turned back to face the inspector. "The gardener added flowers, paths, and fruit trees," she said softly. "He made it a beautiful place for children to go. He left clues to discover delicious fruits. We learned about the fruit of the Holy Spirit, too."

"Papa, what Charlotte Masson is saying is true," Louise said. "There *is* a garden planted among the firs." Charlotte was surprised that Louise would stick up for her—and for Olivier. Louise's father's face turned pink.

Thérèse stepped forward. "The gardener has made a wonderful gift. He wants children to play on his land. Monsieur Bouchard, you gave him the land. Is that right?"

With everyone looking at him, Louise's father began to change his mind—at least somewhat. "You can let the boy out of jail. I give my permission for the children to visit a few more times to play and pick some fruit while we sort all this out," the land-owner said.

Charlotte felt like she could float. She was so happy that she didn't hear the part about visiting just a few times more. "Now we need to get Olivier out of that jail cell!"

Charlotte kept trying to see over the inspector's shoulder as he walked, keys rattling, toward the cell.

When Inspector Dufour opened the door, Olivier stayed with his back against the far wall.

"It's all right, boy. I'm letting you go," the inspector said.

Looking all around and taking uncertain steps, Olivier walked toward them. He shivered when he took his last step out of the cell. Charlotte grabbed Olivier's hand and pulled him alongside her. She showed him the purse, and he took the frog back with a half-smile.

As they walked outside, Charlotte's brother, Theo, ran up to them.

"Theo!" Madame Masson gasped, "What are you doing here?"

"I brought Papa! I told him about the two boys in trouble."

Charlotte's father followed. "A storm is coming."

Olivier looked at the sky. "It's getting dark. I have to find Marc—*now*!"

A Race Against the Storm

∼ 21 ∼

"We can use my carriage," Louise said. "I've already asked my father. He has gone back inside to talk with the inspector. He'll join us later."

Charlotte's mother said, "I'll take Theo home."

"I will pray that you find Marc, and that everything turns out just the way God wants it to be. Prayer is my part of your mission," said Thérèse. As Thérèse said this, Charlotte felt stronger, like she could run all the way to Louise's house. Thérèse turned to walk home.

Charlotte, Charlotte's father, Olivier, Anne, and Louise dashed up onto the glossy, black benches of the carriage. "Go to my house! Quickly, please!" Louise said to the driver, who sat outside. Two bay-colored horses, brown with black manes, started off with a jolt.

Louise turned to Olivier. "I am so sorry. I told my father you were in the garden picking fruit. I hope you can forgive me." She handed him his cap.

"Louise tried to fix her mistake at the courthouse," Charlotte said.

"I forgive you," Oliver said simply. "You're helping now. That's what matters."

The wind pushed against the dark-red curtains of the carriage. Raindrops struck the roof. In no time, their beat tapped even faster than the horses' hooves. Charlotte imagined that the horses were trying to run toward the last light between the clouds, but the storm had taken over the whole sky. *Please let Marc be safe*, she prayed.

A flash of light zapped through the curtains' edges and thunder boomed. As the frightened horses neighed, the carriage slammed to a stop. The children were thrown back against their seats.

Louise gripped the side of the carriage but called to the horses to calm them. The wheels moved again.

They came to the barn. "Where's the stable boy?" asked the driver.

"Maybe he's helping somewhere else," said Louise. "I'll take off the harnesses with you." Charlotte was amazed to see Louise begin caring for the tired and soaked horses. As she worked, mud splashed all over her dress. "Go to the garden and find Marc! I'll stay back and get warm drinks and blankets ready."

Charlotte's father, Monsieur Masson, turned to her and said, "Help Louise in the kitchen. I'll go with the boy into the storm."

"No Papa, I want to go," Charlotte said. "I'm a fast runner. And I know the garden best."

Olivier, Monsieur Masson, and Charlotte ran toward the garden.

The grass was slick with rain. The storm and dusk made every tree look the same. Flower petals blew past.

"Where are the lilies?" Charlotte shouted. "What if they've been torn apart? We won't be able to find the garden door!"

Olivier plunged into the trees. It was the wrong place, and he dashed right and left. Charlotte could only see low, by the lantern light her father carried. She saw the flower path and screamed out to Olivier.

The gray trunks of the beech trees looked like gravestones.

Charlotte and her father followed Olivier's hunched shoulders and his brown cap.

The path ended at the fir trees, which muffled the sound of the storm. The dense green branches caught the rain, carried it down the stems, and split it into thousands of tiny rivers.

"This way, Papa." They passed the place of the Mary doll, the nest box, and at last came to the swing.

"Marc, where are you?" Charlotte called out. Rain had washed away any footprints. Lightning lit up the ladder, but then, the forest went dark.

Olivier jumped to the second rung. "This is where I left him, near the swing." Olivier began to climb. A clatter rang out above, and a branch fell, dagger sharp. It landed close.

"No, boy, stop," Charlotte's father said. "It's dangerous in the lightning." He reached up and pulled Olivier down.

"But what if Marc climbed up here? He loves the swing. He wanted to go on it by himself. Marc!" Olivier shouted his brother's name more loudly than the falling rain.

Charlotte crouched low and looked around. *Please let him be nearby*, she prayed. It was getting darker. Ahead, she spotted an even deeper green. Some time before, the trees had twisted and folded over. Their branches had formed the roof of a shelter, almost like a cave. "Maybe Marc is in here!"

<h1 style="text-align:center">~ 22 ~</h1>

Charlotte cupped her hands around her mouth to call the young boy. Then she listened.

"Charlotte?" a little voice called.

"Olivier! Papa!" said Charlotte. "I can hear him! This way!" She plunged through the twisted branches. Soft needles and bits of moss had fallen on the dirt floor. Inside it was mostly dry, even in the storm.

"Look, baby deer live here!" said a small voice. A hand reached out to her.

She could see a glimpse of fur and the gleam of a large eye in the corner. It was a fawn. The mother deer, however, wasn't there. Charlotte hugged Marc.

"I prayed to God to help me," the younger boy said, "and he did. When the baby deer came in, I felt safe. I wasn't alone."

"No, Marc. No one is ever alone in the Garden for Children," Charlotte said.

Marc tugged on her hand with his much smaller one. "I think pirates hid something back here."

"Olivier has been telling you too many stories. There aren't any pirates in Lisieux." Olivier and Charlotte's father were calling out to them. "We're safe. Come in here!" Charlotte answered.

"But wait, you have to see something Charlotte," the smaller boy said. "I'll show you. It's a tunnel."

At the back of the wall, Charlotte felt like she was in a chapel without candles. But when she felt around in the dark, she found a gap in the leaves. With faith, she pushed her arm forward and felt emptiness. "I think you're right. There *is* a tunnel! But I don't think a pirate built it. Maybe it's another thing the gardener did. We'll take a good look at it tomorrow, when the storm is over."

Charlotte took Marc to the front of the shelter and his worried older brother. Charlotte's father stood behind Olivier. His lantern cast some light into the dark space.

"I'm so sorry that I had to leave you behind," Olivier said. Trying to take Marc's mind off things, he added, "We'll let the frog go now."

Olivier took the frog out of his pocket. Almost nothing glowed in the stormy forest. But the frog, skin glistening, had become wet and shiny. Charlotte watched as the two brothers picked a large, safe puddle for its home.

Soaking wet, the children and Monsieur Masson made their way back to the Bouchard's house. Charlotte's father carried Marc.

Louise and Anne had made warm tea and bread with jam. As a surprise, Louise had found the gardener to join them. Elena had arranged an apricot, a clementine, and a red currant blossom in a bowl. She winked at the children when their eyes lit up as they each saw the fruit. The gardener's face glowed with all the children around. As Marc fell asleep, the elderly man looked toward the fruit. "Where's the pear?"

"There isn't one," Elena said.

"The pear is missing. One tree left," the gardener said. "I can't ever seem to find it."

Charlotte jumped up to show him the map. But Monsieur Dubois only looked confused. He didn't remember anything else.

"Elena, get someone to take the youngest boy and Gardener Dubois back to his cottage," Monsieur Bouchard ordered from the doorway. "You stay in the kitchen."

23

Louise's father stepped into the room.

"Papa, thank you for helping to get Olivier out of jail." Louise stood up and hugged her father.

Olivier said thank you with his head bowed down.

"I'm proud of you, Charlotte, but don't say anything here," Charlotte's father whispered to her. He stood up and shook Monsieur Bouchard's hand. "I know my daughter can be too bold sometimes."

"Being bold is good in a son. But you should be careful to make sure your daughter becomes more ladylike."

"Yes, that is wise advice," Monsieur Masson said. Charlotte's face burned red. Louise sat back down, her hands in her lap. She had changed her clothes and combed her hair so that not one strand was out of place, even after she had helped with the horses.

Monsieur Bouchard turned to Olivier. "You can pick all the fruit that you want from that garden. You are welcome to take it to your family."

"Thank you sir," he said. "That would be a great help."

Monsieur Bouchard turned to everyone else. "But then, I'll be cutting down the trees. I've talked to Monsieur Dubois, and he doesn't even remember that land. I've done what I can to care for him in his old age. Now I need to sell the wood from the trees to pay for someone to take care of him. I've walked through the gardener's land. It's not a real garden. All you've found are three fruit trees."

Charlotte started to speak but stopped when her father gave her a look.

"Yes, I'm sure the children understand," Monsieur Masson said.

Louise looked straight ahead, her face not changing. One tear formed in the corner of Charlotte's eye. Anne hugged herself in a ball. *I have to say something. It's not fair that we aren't allowed to speak*, Charlotte thought. She clenched her fists.

"But there is much more in this garden!" Charlotte said. "Children can learn about the fruits of the Holy Spirit there."

Monsieur Bouchard only shook his head.

"That's enough, Charlotte," Monsieur Masson said. "It's generous of Monsieur Bouchard to allow Olivier to gather some fruit. We don't want anyone getting in trouble again. That's the important thing." The men spoke some more, but nothing changed.

Monsieur Bouchard's men would start to cut down the trees in just one week.

Everyone left the room. Charlotte met Elena, who was standing in the hall, just outside the doorway.

"I overheard everything," Elena said quietly and gave Charlotte a hug. "You will save the garden somehow. I know that's what the gardener wants, even though he can't say it himself."

"I wish Monsieur Dubois remembered more about the garden. Then *he* could say something to save it."

"The gardener can't tell us his own stories," Elena said. "But we can get to know more about him by being in his garden. I am praying that you and the children can save it. Thérèse is praying too, isn't she?"

A happier thought bubbled up in the sadness. "Elena, I've wondered. How did the map get into the library at the school?"

The young maid smiled. "Someone who knows the gardener must have put it there. Someone who wanted someone to find the garden. Maybe a girl like you, who knows how special it is."

"Did you put the map there?" asked Charlotte. Elena only smiled.

Charlotte had only let one tear drop while others were around. But in the dark carriage on the way home, she cried. *How could Monsieur Bouchard say the Garden for Children isn't a real garden? To me, it is the most beautiful garden in the world. But what can I do now?*

The Last Tree

～ 24 ～

The next day, Charlotte, Anne, Olivier, Marc, and Thérèse set out to find the last fruit tree: pear. They had invited Thérèse, because, by praying, she had been part of the mission too. Thérèse was glad to know that Marc was safe and that the younger children had already found three of the trees.

Charlotte shuffled her feet. "I promised Louise she could join us today."

"I'm glad you did, Charlotte. Remember what you said at the jail. It's a garden for *all* children," Thérèse said. "A garden needs all types of flowers to be colorful. And groups of friends need many different personalities to have fun . . . maybe even to find the last tree! Just be what God wants you to be. And let others do the same."

"Well, Louise would want to be the brightest, showiest flower of all," Charlotte said. Thérèse and Anne laughed.

"And what would a garden be like without at least some flowers like that?" Thérèse asked, smiling. Charlotte stopped for a moment to think.

Charlotte often felt angry at Louise for singing and showing off and for always competing with her. But the night before, Louise had been quiet when it mattered most. She had said nothing to her father about protecting the garden.

Right then, Louise rushed out of her house. Her eyes looked red.

Charlotte looked at Louise's sad face. She knew that even her own father hadn't said anything the night before.

"I love the garden so much," Louise said. "I am sorry for what happened to Olivier. I made a terrible mistake."

"I've tried to do good things in the garden, but I was wrong, too!" Charlotte said. "I know in my heart that I shouldn't have left you out, Louise. I'm sorry. I'd like to try to be friends."

"I'd like to be friends, too. Perhaps we can save the garden together. I don't want this to be one of our last days there."

Thérèse looked back and forth between the girls. "One of the last days? Why? What is happening?"

Charlotte told her about Monsieur Bouchard's plans to cut down the trees. While Olivier grabbed hold of one of the tree trunks, Louise looked down to the ground.

"It's not your fault, Louise," Anne said. "I don't think there is anything you could have said to make your father change his mind."

Thérèse hugged Louise, Charlotte, and Anne. "Charlotte, you've done so much to find the trees on the map. All of you know that Monsieur Dubois planted a true garden."

"Our mother loved the fruit from here," said Olivier.

"This garden has deer and a swing!" Marc added.

"Children can see this, but most adults can't." Thérèse looked around thoughtfully. "It is almost like . . . children have a special faith in Jesus that helps them see things adults don't."

Thérèse looked at the map Charlotte was holding. "We must show adults like Monsieur Bouchard that the Garden for Children is a real garden."

"The last tree is marked 'treasure.' Maybe that will help," Charlotte said.

"Let's pray that we can find something there to help us," Thérèse said. "Something full of wonder!"

Louise smiled and spun. Once again hopeful, Charlotte leaped as high as she could. Back on the ground, Charlotte said, "When I first found the map, I thought the treasure might be a jewel. I wanted to sew it on a dress." With everyone staring at her, she turned red.

"That's all right," Louise said. "That's what I thought just now."

"Now I only want the treasure to be something that can save the garden," Charlotte said. "Come this way to a tunnel Marc found during the storm. It might lead us to the last tree."

"Thérèse and Louise, each tree is a virtue," Anne said. "The others were love, gentleness, and joy. This last pear tree will be patience."

"Were those the different kinds of fruit you told me about?" Louise asked.

"Those are fruits of the Holy Spirit," Thérèse said.

As they arrived in the garden, the children headed toward the baby deer's shelter. In the daylight, the friends could see a thick, tall hedge behind the twisted trees. Charlotte wondered what was behind that hedge. The tunnel at the back of the shelter seemed to be the only way in.

Charlotte heard a frog croaking in the coolness and quiet. Was it the one the boys had let go?

"How is this place about patience?" Louise wondered.

Marc scrunched his face. "I had to wait a long time. Olivier said to stay here, near the swing."

"Some animals sleep all winter in caves," Anne said. "That's also patience."

Marc scrambled in first. Charlotte and the others followed.

Once they entered the tunnel, Thérèse pointed to white stones on the ground. On each stone the gardener had painted acorns.

"Small acorns patiently turn into oak trees that live many years," Thérèse said.

"I see light!" Marc yelled.

Then he disappeared.

25

The children rushed after Marc through the tunnel. Charlotte didn't want to lose him again.

On the other end, they found a colorful, calico garden—a round meadow dotted with bright-red poppies, yellow-centered daisies, and Thérèse's favorite . . .

"Cornflowers!" Thérèse and Charlotte shouted together.

"Now this looks like a real, planted garden of flowers!" Louise said.

"But the tree . . ." Olivier said and stopped midway.

In the center, a gray tree trunk had twisted with the wind. One branch had split and fallen, pinned in the ground. Dead leaves, coated in a ghost-colored powder, turned their backs to the sky. A single ring of six green leaves sheltered the one and only blossom that opened to the sun.

"It's almost dead," said Anne with a voice as fragile as the tree's branches. Olivier looked at her sadly with his gray eyes.

"Maybe there is something we can do to help the tree," Louise said. "But, this is still a tree surrounded with flowers. It's the kind of thing you see in every garden. Maybe my father will change his mind!"

Olivier sunk to his knees. "But do you think we'll be able to save the tree?"

"It's so small," said Anne.

"That's why Gardener Dubois couldn't find it. We *will* save it—with the help of Jesus. Then, it will grow to be like the others, and we'll show the gardener," Charlotte said with strength.

"This tree truly stands for patience," Thérèse said. "Olivier, we will pray that it will be all right. And let's all pray for the health of Olivier's and Marc's mother. Lord Jesus, if it be your will, please heal their mother. And comfort her and her family in this illness. Amen."

The children were silent for a moment in the peace around them.

Louise danced toward some tall hedges. Charlotte followed.

Louise touched a bud on a branch. "I do love this garden, too."

Charlotte looked beyond her. "There is a small building behind this hedge!"

Calling the others over, they started breaking branches. They all worked until they uncovered the door to a playhouse.

"My brother, Theo, would love to play here," Charlotte said.

Then they stopped. On the door, there was a sign. Charlotte couldn't believe what it said: "Louise and Vincent."

Had the gardener left it there? Had he really meant everything to be just for the Bouchard children after all? Charlotte thought to herself.

Louise traced the letters. "We'll add the names of everyone who visits. This playhouse is part of the garden, and the garden is for *all* children. Look how happy we are here! The gardener couldn't have imagined all of us when he built this." Louise danced away.

Charlotte said only to Anne, "We wanted to find the treasure marked on the map, at the pear tree. Now I think I know what it is."

"What is it?" Anne asked.

"We need to tell Monsieur Bouchard," Charlotte said.

"It'll be dusk soon. Let's get him," Anne said.

Olivier and Louise came up to them. "Look at all we've found," Olivier said. "Do you think it's enough to prove that the garden is real?"

"Yes, look around, the flowers, the playhouse," Louise said. "It has to be enough. I'll go and bring him."

Louise disappeared through the tunnel. The others waited. The only sounds were birds singing and leaves twisting in the breeze. The children didn't talk. Charlotte prayed. *Help Monsieur Bouchard see that the playhouse and flowers make this a real garden, one worth saving.*

~ 26 ~

At last, Charlotte heard Louise's voice. "It really is this way, Papa."

"I can barely fit through here," her father said.

"It's a tunnel in a garden for children," Louise said. "But it *is* a true garden. You'll see."

Monsieur Bouchard, Louise, and Charlotte's father stepped into the late afternoon light.

"Welcome, Papa and Monsieur Masson, to the hidden flower garden and pear tree," Louise announced. "This is the center of the Garden for Children."

"And there is a playhouse with a real tile roof," Charlotte said. "The gardener wrote the names of your children here."

"I can clear the branches from around the walls," Olivier said. "I can work to clean everything up."

From the other side of the pear tree, Anne said, "Cornflowers grow here."

"Monsieur Bouchard?" Thérèse asked politely. "Do you see that the children have discovered a true garden?"

"Children, you are too hopeful. That tree will never grow fruit," Monsieur Bouchard said. "Yes, there are some things here, an old playhouse and flowers with weeds. It's not a true garden, though. There isn't anything especially beautiful here. It's all ordinary."

"But Jesus loves what's ordinary," Thérèse said. "This garden is full of God's love."

"The more we give from the garden, the more beautiful the garden seems to grow," Charlotte said.

"Animals like deer and birds are safe here," Anne said.

"I've picked fruit here," Olivier said. "When I come back, there is always more fruit. It's made my mama so happy. Please."

"It's made me happy, too," Louise said. "It's a beautiful garden. Why can't you see, Papa?"

"Maybe he can't see because he's a grown-up," Marc whispered.

"Louise, we have many beautiful gardens already," Monsieur Bouchard said.

"Not like this one," Louise said. "This is the Garden for Children."

"There *is* treasure in this garden," Charlotte said. "We've found it here at the pear tree. I thought I'd find a jewel, but instead I found friends—true friends."

Charlotte rushed to hold Louise's hand on one side and Anne's on the other. All of the other children ran to hold hands so that they all linked together. The boys ran to each end. Thérèse smiled the most.

Charlotte could feel the love of friendship flowing through the chain. Love was the first fruit of the Holy Spirit that she and Anne had found. *We have all become more loving, gentle, joyful, and patient*, Charlotte thought. *We have been growing the fruits of the Holy Spirit in our hearts all along.*

"We cannot disappoint these children," Charlotte's father said.

"I remember the friends I had as a child. Seeing my daughter with friends like these around her, I can believe in the garden, too," said Monsieur Bouchard. "We'll keep the garden, Louise. I won't cut any of the trees down."

The loud cheering made the men step back.

Charlotte turned to Thérèse. "It's getting dark. But nothing will break this chain. We'll come back every chance we can!" The fathers stood aside, smiling as the children excitedly chattered around them.

"Charlotte, I leave for Carmel on April ninth," Thérèse said. "Once I enter that place of prayer, I'll remain there for the rest of my life."

"But that's in just a few days!" Charlotte said.

Thérèse looked down. "I'm sorry, Charlotte, but today is my last chance to be in the garden. I must visit with my family now until I leave home."

Charlotte could see the garden filling only with shadows. Another petal fell from the pear tree.

"Your last chance?" Louise said, overhearing. She quickly pulled the other children toward her. "Thérèse isn't coming back here. We need to think of goodbye gifts."

Thérèse waited. Monsieur Bouchard and Charlotte's father listened to the plans.

A few moments later, Louise bowed in front of Thérèse. "My gift is a dance." Her arms bent like grass in the wind, and her legs jumped like a fawn's in summer. Even Monsieur Bouchard came forward and added a waltz step by himself.

Olivier sprung in front just as Louise finished. "My gift is three cartwheels." He turned as fast as bicycle wheels spinning. Marc did one to add to his brother's. Monsieur Masson clapped and cheered.

Anne had been working on something off to the side. "For my gift, I've made you a wreath of wild-flowers." She handed them carefully to Thérèse.

Charlotte walked to Thérèse. "Every time I think of you, especially when we are in the garden, I will pray for you. And I'll give you the special blue velvet purse that I made."

Thérèse hugged her friends. "I'll remember these thoughtful gifts always. Each one is different, just like each of you."

Charlotte looked at Thérèse one last time.

"Even though I won't be here, I'll always be part of the friendship chain that we made when we held hands," Thérèse said to her. "I could never forget you, Charlotte. I'll remember you when I pray. I'll ask Jesus always to help you live with love."

Epilogue

A Return Home

As Charlotte got off the train in Lisieux, the silent winter sky had turned the color of ice. Still, Charlotte felt full of hope. Now sixteen years old, Charlotte had been attending a school for girls in Paris with Louise and Anne. In the evenings, they had walked on grand streets lit up to show the way to beautiful cafés. But in late February, in a city garden, Charlotte had found a tiny white flower blooming. She knew that she had to return home to Lisieux and the Garden for Children.

Charlotte hurried down the street. In her purse, she had placed an important list. The garden had been the start of her doing small, good things. She needed to find that way again. In the garden, she had understood God's gentle love for her and discovered how much she wanted to love others. People spoke greetings to her, but she didn't even hear them. She was almost running, her boots tapping on the cobblestones.

She crossed the Bouchard estate. The petals of the orange lilies had disappeared, but she found the door anyway. Charlotte took one step after another on the old path.

But as she came to the fir trees, she saw a young man.

He wore a black woolen coat. He took off his hat, showing dark brown hair, and turned toward her. His gray eyes were open wide in hope. He stood so much taller than she did now.

"Charlotte?" he said.

"Olivier! You've come back to the garden, too."

"It seemed that we weren't finished," he said.

"Because the garden isn't." Charlotte opened the piece of paper she had in her purse. "Finding the trees, we became more loving, joyful. . . ."

"Patient and gentle," Olivier said, finishing the list. "The four fruits of the dove, the Holy Spirit. I'll never forget them."

"But Olivier, there are five more! Peace, kindness, generosity, faithfulness, and self-control."

"Do you know what that means?" Olivier asked, his eyes bright. "We have the chance to plant five more fruit trees."

"And set out five more paths with painted stones. I guess it's up to us to continue what the gardener began," Charlotte said, smiling. Five snowflakes flurried in front of her face. "When spring arrives, we can start."

Charlotte and Olivier walked to the center of the garden and through the tunnel. A partridge flew into the safety of the winter pear tree, which had grown many branches. The two garden protectors kept walking, checking the trees where fruit would grow again.

As they left, more snow began to drift in the wind, writing lacy scrollwork across the garden door. Charlotte and Olivier would open it again in spring.

Charlotte remembered the last time she had seen Thérèse. Praying for her friend as she had promised, she could almost feel Thérèse's presence again. As she looked up, the snow seemed to fall in spirals of white roses—with love.

Historical Note

The Search for the Hidden Garden is fiction, but the end of the book is true. Thérèse Martin really did enter a Carmelite monastery at the age of fifteen in 1888 in Lisieux, France. The story of her life would have remained hidden and been soon forgotten, just like the garden almost did, but her older sister, Pauline, asked Thérèse to write her life down in a journal. Her writings became a book called *Story of a Soul*. She wrote the book in three parts, and filled it with stories of her life that she told at different times to different people. In all three parts, the last word she wrote was "love."

Inside a small convent, Thérèse didn't have a chance to do grand, heroic things. Instead, she

decided to do small, loving things. She chose to be nicest to nuns who weren't her best friends.

Thérèse still trusted in God even when she became sick with tuberculosis, a serious disease. Thérèse wanted her soul to become like a child, trusting and loving. She wanted to find a Little Way to follow Jesus. As she became weaker, Thérèse still did everything with love. Just before she died, at the age of twenty-four, she promised to spend eternity in heaven doing good on earth and to send roses to those who ask her to pray for them. Saint Thérèse is known by those who love her as "The Little Flower."

Discussion Questions

1. Have you ever decided to leave someone out like Charlotte left Louise out of the garden? Or like Anne, have you ever seen someone else do this? What could they have done differently?

2. In this story, sometimes the adults told Charlotte she was too bold. Do you think that both girls and boys today have the freedom to be themselves? Why or why not?

3. Charlotte and her friends learned about love, gentleness, joy, and patience. Pick one of these virtues and explain how a character in the story showed that virtue.

4. Did any characters change in the story? If they did, how did they change and why?

5. After she died, Thérèse was made a saint. The Church gives us saints to show us how to follow Jesus. How would you describe a saint now that you've read about Thérèse?

6. How would the story have been different if Charlotte had told Louise about the map in the beginning?

7. Draw your idea of the gardener's map to the Garden for Children.

8. The gardener made a beautiful garden, but many people had forgotten about what he had done. Are there people in your community who are forgotten or not thanked, such as a custodian at your school or a cafeteria worker? Write a thank you note to a person like this.

9. At the end of the story, Charlotte and her friends gave gifts showing their talents to Thérèse. What gift would you give?

Acknowledgments

I wish to thank Jaymie Stuart Wolfe, who introduced me to Saint Thérèse as an inspiration and guided the project so beautifully according to the saint's Little Way. I am grateful to my daughter, Laura, who loves birds, fir trees, and gardens. My mother, Cheryl, shared many stories of her lively childhood, which helped me to imagine Charlotte's adventures and bold character. My uncle, David Davis, was an inspiration for the character of Monsieur Dubois, who planted a landscape of play and faith for children. Uncle Dave created a multi-track model train display, featuring houses, trees, and hills, simply for local children and adults to enjoy in Athens County, Ohio.

I want to thank Laura Smith, Makena Weberski, Katherine Mak, and Silver Stars skaters, girls who read early versions of the story and thought of ideas about the garden. From France, Genevieve Sauvage-Smith, a native French speaker fluent in English, helped me to understand the culture and the landscape, the setting that shaped the novel and Thérèse's spirituality. I hope that readers enjoy discovering the Garden for Children, planted with many of the flowers, trees, and prayers that Thérèse mentioned in her writings.

Sherry Weaver Smith

became Catholic after working alongside Salesian Sisters who were dedicated to helping homeless and working children in Manila, the Philippines. After marrying her husband, Michael, Sherry wrote her first poems and children's fiction for their daughter, Laura. Sherry's haiku collection, *Land Shapes*, has been published by Richer Resources Publications. Sherry has also worked in various product management and grant-writing positions for healthcare companies and nonprofit organizations. She received her bachelor's degree in math and East Asian studies from Duke University, and a master's in politics from the University of Oxford, England. Sherry's adventures with Pauline Kids include *The Wolf and the Shield* (2016) and *Search for the Hidden Garden* (2016).

Friends *with the* SAINTS

Meet the saints

in their own times and places. Discover the gift of their friendship here and now.

Pauline
BOOKS & MEDIA

The Daughters of St. Paul operate book and media centers at the following addresses. Visit, call, or write the one nearest you today, or find us at www.paulinestore.org.

CALIFORNIA
3908 Sepulveda Blvd, Culver City, CA 90230   310-397-8676
935 Brewster Avenue, Redwood City, CA 94063   650-369-4230

FLORIDA
145 S.W. 107th Avenue, Miami, FL 33174   305-559-6715

HAWAII
1143 Bishop Street, Honolulu, HI 96813   808-521-2731

ILLINOIS
172 North Michigan Avenue, Chicago, IL 60601   312-346-4228

LOUISIANA
4403 Veterans Memorial Blvd, Metairie, LA 70006   504-887-7631

MASSACHUSETTS
885 Providence Hwy, Dedham, MA 02026   781-326-5385

MISSOURI
9804 Watson Road, St. Louis, MO 63126   314-965-3512

NEW YORK
64 W. 38th Street, New York, NY 10018   212-754-1110

SOUTH CAROLINA
243 King Street, Charleston, SC 29401   843-577-0175

TEXAS
Currently no book center; for parish exhibits or outreach evangelization, contact: 210-569-0500, or SanAntonio@paulinemedia.com, or P.O. Box 761416, San Antonio, TX 78245

VIRGINIA
1025 King Street, Alexandria, VA 22314   703-549-3806

CANADA
3022 Dufferin Street, Toronto, ON M6B 3T5   416-781-9131

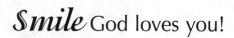

Smile God loves you!